Chapter 1

Coincidences are mostly just that, and you think no more about them. They are not connected meaningfully, nor are you meant to experience them for some higher reason or purpose. When I saw the guy with the hooked nose I had little idea that I would meet him again and be dragged into a murder mystery in Paris. That particular coincidence certainly had consequences for me.

We were both in the queue to view the Turin Shroud, or Santa Sindone, the name by which the locals in Torino know it. They bring it out on special occasions from the specially built Baroque chapel adjoining the Cathedral, where it is normally kept in a wooden and silver box. Hordes of people come to see it, the curious, devout Catholics, and the people like me who write about it. The last expositions were in 2010 and 2015 with another due in 2025.

My name is Max Quillan and I am a historian specialising in French medieval history. The topic on which I usually write is the Cathars, a sect in South West France who were exterminated in the thirteenth century by the Catholic Church. They were largely forgotten until Kate Mosse wrote novels about them and the tourism people in Occitanie started using 'Cathar country' as a marketing tool. I got interested because my surname is the same as the name of a town in the area.

Everyone knows about the Turin Shroud and it was after I had written about it for a popular history journal that I found myself with an invitation to take part in a symposium on the Shroud during its exhibition.

This took the form of an Any Questions panel in English organised by the Waldensian church, another sect from the same period as the Cathars. (In the case of the Waldensians, think low church protestants, although they predated the Reformation by a couple of hundred years). They were luckier than the Cathars and escaped extermination by hiding in the Piedmont valleys. These days they have a higher profile because many Italians whether believers of not, vote for the proportion of their taxes earmarked for religions to go to them rather than the Vatican.

The panel discussion was not part of the official Shroud exhibition. It took place in the Tempio Valdese in the Corsa V. Emmanuelle II, their largest church, a domed building which proclaims grandeur from a distance but inside is as unadorned as a non-conformist chapel. The event had been organised by the senior Waldensian pastor as his way of saying 'there's more to religion than a piece of cloth'. In a spirit of ecumenism he gave two places on the panel to a couple of believers in the authenticity of the Shroud. The other two panelists were sceptics of whom I was the less fervent. The case for the Shroud was made by a forensic scientist and an expert who had been part of a panel which had run tests on the cloth. Both were laymen and practising Roman Catholics.

The other sceptic and myself had been accommodated in spartan flats in a building for Waldensian pastors behind the Tempio. The Italian scientist and lay Catholic were the guests of a local Monsignor with very conservative views. The scientist turned out to be a zealot who clashed bitterly with my fellow sceptic, an American brought over to support the findings of a microbiologist in 1978 that the image on the Shroud had been painted on with pigment dissolved in gelatin. The Yank was also an expert on radio carbon dating and the scientists took up most of the time in ill-tempered exchanges. An auxiliary Bishop of Torino had surprisingly agreed to say a few words at the start and even more surprisingly was even-handed in his contribution. He was canny enough to keep any of his clergy from slugging it out on the panel. That would be bad for PR although I knew that there were many Catholics who shuddered at the parade of relics of which their church has plenty. The diplomatic prelate seemed to me to be saying 'If it helps your faith to believe in the authenticity of the Shroud, then go ahead'. He managed to avoid stating categorically the Shroud was actually used to wrap the body of Jesus. Perhaps like me he believed it was a clever medieval forgery and coming along to the panel discussion provided a way to secretly distance himself from it.

My role in the discussion was to outline how the Shroud surfaced in 1354 when it was exhibited in Lirey, a village in North-Central France. As was common at the time with other relics, it was a good source of income from the pilgrims who came to view it. The shroud was denounced as a forgery by the bishop of Troyes in 1389, and passed to the House of Savoy who took it to Chambery where it was damaged by fire in 1453. In 1578, the Savoys moved the shroud to their new capital in Turin. I tried not to be too boring with the history or too scathing about the way relics were used as cash generators in medieval times. In reviewing the historical context I could not resist mentioning that the 1988 carbon dating process had established that the linen of the Shroud was 95% certain to date from 1300 BCE plus or minus fifty years. That earned me a hostile glare from the two Catholic apologists.

The debate at times became acrimonious not only between the scientists, but between the Waldensian chairman and the pious lay Catholic. Frankly the whole thing solved nothing except to provide a more civilised form of religious punch-up than the religious wars which were my bread and butter as a historian. As I was leaving the Tempio the Bishop took me aside and asked smilingly if I was a Catholic.

"Not guilty," I replied, returning his smile. "I'm actually Presbyterian from my mother's side. Non-practising now." It seemed churlish to add non-believing.

"I just wanted to say I enjoyed your book on the Cathars. Not all of us Catholics think that those who think differently should be beaten into conformity or burned."

"Thanks," I replied. "Our Italian scientist friend might not agree with you."

"I think you're right," he conceded with a wry smile and quickly changed the subject. He knew I had arrived only that afternoon. "Have you seen the Shroud yet? You know there is only tomorrow and Sunday left for the public display? There is a mass of thanksgiving on Sunday night and if you want, I can let you see it when they bring it back from the Cathedral into the Chapel on Monday morning before they seal it back in the chest."

It was Friday evening and my train seat was already booked to go to Paris on Saturday. I politely declined his offer and said I would take the chance to stand in the queue in the morning. Believing what I did about the origins of the Shroud, or rather not believing, I still thought it would look rather strange, even arrogant, if I had traveled all that way and not bothered to take a look. The symposium had not proved anything nor had been worth the long journey.

I wished I had arranged to have more time in Torino, once the jewel in the Savoy crown, but I needed to be in Paris that weekend. On Monday I was due to start a series of summer vacation courses I was giving on the Albigensian Crusade (i.e. the suppression of Catharism) at the Sorbonne. A rented apartment awaited me in the Opera -Montmartre district,

otherwise known as the 9th Arondissement and I had yet to
see it. No one showed any sign of inviting me to dine out (or
even in) when the panel discussion ended. I guess I had
proved myself too heretical for the believers and too boring
for the sceptics. I escaped to the hard mattress of my
bedroom. From the window there was a sideways view of the
Synagogue outside which an armoured car was stationed to
ward off jihadists. So much for having moved on since the
Middle Ages.

After a meager breakfast on what had been provided in the
fridge of my flat, I joined the long queue to see the Shroud.
It started in a park amid trees which gave some shade in the
morning sun then passed round the back of the cathedral to a
long ramp of plastic flooring protected from the glare by
awning. The air temperature was rising faster than the queue
was moving. I kept myself distracted from worrying whether
I would make it into the cathedral before my train departed
just after 3pm, by plugging earphones into my mobile and
listening to Spotify. I could allow myself thirty minutes to
walk up Corsa V. Emmanuelle to the railway station after
collecting my case back at the flat behind the Tempio.

When I eventually entered the cathedral there was still plenty
of time. It was then that I noticed a man with a hooked nose
and a sour expression, several metres ahead of me in the
queue. His solid physique looked as if he could have been a
bouncer or bodyguard. Medium height, swarthy complexion

and all muscle. There was something about him that made me look at him twice. Perhaps it was his hard cruel eyes, slits beneath a shiny bald head. More likely it was because he directed them away from where everyone else was looking. They settled for a moment on me and it was obvious they did not belong to a saintly person. Everyone else looked towards the Shroud as they came into the darkened nave, but he looked around as if he was looking for something else. I must confess it crossed my mind then that he might be about to make some some kind of protest but it didn't happen. He was wearing chinos and a pink short- sleeved shirt, so a suicide vest could be ruled out. Besides, our queue was being monitored by men in yellow vests who were presumably there as security. Shortly after entering the nave we were split into two streams. The handicapped in wheelchairs and their carers continued at ground level and passed closer to the Shroud which was stretched out behind an altar rail. The rest of us went up a wooden ramp to a higher vantage point to look across and down at the 4.4 by 1.1 metres of linen bearing the mysterious image.

Anguished cries and sobs suddenly broke the pious silence. Some of the handicapped people passing close to the Shroud were so moved by what they thought was the burial cloth of Christ that they were venting intense emotions. Rather loudly. The experience obviously meant much to them. Normally I would have been moved by the sight of handicapped people in emotional distress but, forgive me, I felt a sense of repulsion. What could this piece of cloth do for them that doctors could not? I caught sight of the Hook Nose. He too was unmoved and was looking away from the Shroud at a door which led from the nave towards the adjoining Chapel. The significance of that stare became apparent only much later.

Chapter 2

Paris was still having one of its frequent 'manifestations' when I arrived just after 9pm. Apparently tear gas had been fired when things turned ugly, as they often did, and some streets were closed. The last thing I needed after a long train journey was to be caught in the middle of placard-waving protesters. When I arrived at Gare de Lyon, fortunately the RER was running normally and I got to Gare du Nord with no problems. My term in Paris as a student had given me a good knowledge of the streets and I walked the rest of the way to my flat in Rue Marronnier. I had been sent a key and the entry code for the door to my home in London by post. Nobody from the University could be bothered to come out and welcome me, certainly not late on a Saturday evening. The flat was owned by a charity which was anxious to maximise its income by renting out to birds of passage like me. Holiday rentals were too much of a hassle and so they had a contract with the Sorbonne to accommodate visiting academics as tenants which gave them a guaranteed income. The concierge was paid a small fee to manage the changeovers and also save the 15% fee an agency would have charged for doing little or nothing. Fully furnished, my flat had two bedrooms and was on the third floor. After my walk from the station I was glad to see an elevator.

Before I could reach it, a door to my right opened and the concierge emerged. Not the dragon of Parisian legends, but a pretty woman in her thirties. Her dark hair was tucked back in a pony-tail. She looked nervously at me and spoke in stilted English.

"Are you by any chance, Doctor Quillan?" she used the French pronunciation of my name – Kee-yong, but spoke with an accent that I could not place. "I was expecting you earlier."

"Sorry. I was delayed by the demonstration and I had to walk some of the way. I had the entry code and the key so I didn't want to bother you. Especially late on a Saturday evening."

"That's all right, I'm here to help and see you get settled. There's a security camera in my flat and I saw you at the door."

"Your English is very good," I said, relieved that I didn't have to deal with the surly Parisian concierge of legend. Knowing that being friends with the concierge was the key to hassle-free apartment life, I added, "Please call me Max. I'm not a real doctor, only a dull academic."

"Thank you. My name is Maria O'Mara. I'm Portuguese but my husband is Irish so we use English at home. He is a lorry driver and is away so I am grateful of the chance to speak English. Some of the other tenants complain my French is not good enough and I knew you were English."

Maria took me up in the lift and showed me how to operate the shutters. No air conditioning of course. There was a printed sheet in various languages about where to find transport links and food shopping.

"There are two apartments on each of the four floors," she explained, "Served by the elevator and main stair around the lift shaft. In addition, on the attic level there are three chambres de bonnes. Do you know what these are?"

"Yes, the servant's quarters," I answered, thinking instantly of La Boheme and tiny bed sits where tiny hands were frozen in Parisian winters. This form of budget bed-sit still lurks beneath the roof of many apartment blocks and provides low-cost accommodation for students and low-paid workers. "I imagine there is a great demand for them."

"There certainly is. Some of the proprietors here wanted to stop people staying in them but two bedrooms are owned by the charity and they wanted to be able to offer affordable accommodation to young people. One is occupied by a nurse from the Cote D'Ivoire." Then she added somewhat unnecessarily, "She's black so you will recognise her. Another is a young Scottish man who works as a steward on the Thalys trains out of Gare du Nord. He's called Nick and is very friendly. The third is a Romanian student who is studying at the Conservatoire but he is away visiting his family in Iasi. I'm telling you all that in case you see them coming in the front door and you think they are intruders. They are not allowed to use the main stair or elevator and have their own wooden stairs at the rear. Some of the proprietors are very strong about security. There is also a set of cellars which you can reach from the bottom of the servants' stair but looking at the luggage you brought, I don't think you'll need it for storage." She smiled, not flirtingly, though she must have been lonely with her *routier* husband on the road so much. Anyway, I was almost twice her age.

She explained that the majority of the occupants of the main apartments were away for the summer. The other flat on my landing was occupied by Madame Lafont, a widow, who never went away but Maria was sure would be pleased if I introduced myself. Another elderly lady in the flat above me was called Madame Adam. Something in the way Maria pronounced the name implied that she would NOT be pleased to meet me. If it was like other apartment blocks I had lived in, people would not be anxious to get to know their neighbours. Paris is Paris.

There was a television set (French channels only) but no landline. I use a data bundle on my mobile for my internet and phone so I had no need of the latter. Maria gave me a card with her mobile number and left me. I went straight to bed.

The next morning I found an eating place round the corner for breakfast which was open on Sunday, and a small food store to tide me over until Monday. As in many of the inner Paris districts there were no large supermarkets near at hand but the small traders somehow still managed to make a living. On the corner beneath my apartment was a *brocante* selling antiques and more of an expensive bric-a-brac called Brocando. I assumed this was a sort of *franglais* pun. The flats were built midway between Gare du Nord and Gare St Lazare in the era when Paris was undergoing a huge rebuild under Baron Haussmann.

I walked up Rue Rochechouart to Pigalle and further uphill to Montmartre and returned to the flat in time to eat the few things I had bought for supper that morning. I had to get to the Sorbonne for nine the next morning to meet my masters and find out what my teaching schedule was to be. I had been promised that my timetable would leave me plenty of opportunity to explore Paris and I had given little thought to what I might do with all this free time. As it turned out I ended up playing detective in the saga of the Shroud, but at this point I had no idea it was about to be stolen or that in consequence a murder would shake the unexceptional life of the apartment block I have just described.

Chapter 3

I should explain that I am a divorcee with no children and the few distant living relatives I have are scattered in the USA and Canada. I did think of inviting some friends to occupy the second bedroom in the apartment and to explore Paris together. Best to wait and see if the Sorbonne duties were as light as they promised. After my term as an undergraduate in Paris, my previous stay in France was in Montpellier where I did my doctorate and thus I know the Occitanie region well. My ex-wife still lives near there but she was hardly likely to want to come to Paris to see the man she had thrown over for an artist. Of course, if this were a novel, a stunning beauty would knock on my door to borrow a cup of sugar and we would watch sunsets in Montmartre. I had introduced myself to my neighbour Mme Lafont after unpacking my groceries. As she was in her eighties and bent double with arthritis the knock was not going to come from that direction.

In the event, the knock did come but it was not from the front door. I was in the kitchen at the back of the property with one window overlooking the courtyard which the block forms with apartments in Rue Rochechouart. In the corner of the kitchen was a door which I assumed was a pantry of sorts. It had been closed with two bolts. The knock was coming from there. It came again, louder. I drew back the bolts and there was a young man standing on the wooden backstair about which Maria had told me. It was Nick the train steward from the attic and he was holding a plastic bag containing food.

"Hello," he announced cheerily in a Scots accent. "I heard from Maria that you were English and arrived late last night. I make a mean waffle - if you like them". He held up the plastic bag which I assumed at first (wrongly) contained waffles. The waffles apparently needed to be assembled and cooked. I twigged this when he asked if I had any baking powder.

"There ought to be some in that cupboard up there," he continued, as if the last thing I would want to do was refuse my chance to eat his waffles. "You see I used to make them for the McKinleys, the American couple who lived here last year. Actually to tell the truth they taught me but in the end mine were better than theirs. I would have made them in my room and brought you down some but my facilities are a bit cramped."

Later in my stay when I had a look at Nick's room, I understood why he couldn't make them there. It had a tiny shower, a sink, a clothes rack and a single bed strewn with a pile of dirty clothes; all jammed into a space no larger than my ex-wife's wardrobe. His friendly manner was difficult to resist and I had nothing better to do, so I invited him in for supper. Popped some more of the frozen chips I had bought into the oven, halved the pork cutlet I had begun to fry and opened a bottle of wine while he got to work on his waffles. Fortunately he had brought eggs and butter since I had neither. He scoured the cupboards for sugar and vanilla essence which by the grace of the McKinleys, he found. By the time he was finished the kitchen was a complete mess.

"I'm not gay," he suddenly announced over his shoulder, as he beat his mixture in a bowl, perhaps to ward off either hostile suspicions or over-friendly moves on my part.

"Neither am I," I felt obliged to reply.

"I just thought as a new tenant you might like some info on the lie of the land here. I may live in the attic but I keep my ear to the ground, if that's not an oxymoron."

Nick was clearly not a moron himself and I wondered what a lad like him was doing working as a steward on a train. It turned out that he was earning enough to save in order to go to university without incurring a loan. The steward job paid well and was augmented by tips which I imagine Nick's persuasive manner elicited easily. His route on the Thalys took him from Paris to Brussels and sometimes on to Amsterdam. The hours he apparently worked were not for a family person and did not leave him much time to socialise. I realised that he was probably lonely and could be a good source of information. As it proved.

"You don't have a car, do you?" he asked.

"No."

"Good. There is an underground garage the next street over but it's very expensive and you have to journey to the centre of the earth down a spiral ramp. The McKinleys used it because they wanted to make trips outside Paris. Leave a car outside in the street and you'll have it dented front and back. The Paris parking method is to squeeze into a space like a dodgem car shunting to and fro."

During my walk I had passed several cars parked tightly bumper to bumper in the streets outside and admired how the drivers had managed to squeeze them in. I had imagined it was some kind of reverse parking software. Now I knew.

"How do you get about then, Nick? I assume you go to Gare du Nord on foot. It's what, ten minutes walk?"

"Indeed I do. I try to avoid the metro. Noisy, dirty and packed like sardines. Buses are OK if you know the routes and they aren't on strike. Personally I take Velib. The white bike scheme. Are you familiar with it?"

I had heard of the scheme but didn't know what it was called.

"20,000 bikes and 1400 docking points in Paris," Nick pursued his sales pitch. "For a few Euros a month you can pick one and drop it within 30 minutes or even use it free for an hour. I use one to go to the Scots Kirk off the Champs Elysees on Sunday mornings. Brilliant. I'm there in less than twenty minutes for nothing. You should try it."

"The church or the bike?" I replied thinking of my Scots mother who would have approved of the former. Nick in his enthusiasm had forgotten our age difference and registering it now, revised his sales pitch.

"Well, I would wait until you have walked some of the Paris streets before I try. See where the pressure points are. The Parisian drivers are not cyclist friendly despite the French Tour de France obsession. Amsterdam is much easier for a bike when I'm there. But if you're worried about the hills, Velib have electric bikes as well." He paused. "Actually, I forgot. There is a bike which goes with your apartment. Chuck McKinley left it behind when they left for America. It's probably in the cellar that belongs to this apartment. I suppose you will have a key."

I said I thought there was such a key hanging in the kitchen. We left it there, with me promising to have a look at the bike. We had finished the pork chops lathered with a tin of baked beans I had found in a cupboard and drunk most of the bottle of wine when Nick produced his waffles and a tiny bottle of maple syrup from his trouser pocket. They were delicious and I told him so. He talked about his work as a steward and it was fascinating to see the job from his perspective. I fished out a bottle of whisky from my luggage which he declined. A Scotsman who didn't drink whisky?

"I don't drink spirits, Max," he explained. "My father was a bad example and I see enough of drunks on the train. But if you have a coffee I wouldn't mind and then I must go. Early shift tomorrow."

I served us both coffee and a dram for myself. I had actually enjoyed his company as he told me a little more about life behind the scenes in our apartment block. Apparently the old woman above me, Madame Adam was a witch who wanted the attic dwellers expelled. The young couple on the same floor, the Fischers, were friendly and trying for a baby (I was mystified how he knew that but he seemed to have a gift for getting people to tell him things as he chattered away himself.). He explained that the old couple on the first floor were away all summer to their home in the Gers and were likely to sell as they could not afford two homes any longer. Across the landing from them was Homer Dieudonné who was something in banking or officialdom and Nick added wittily, as his name implied, considered himself God's gift and did not even say '*bonjour*' to other proprietors (a real no-no in French manners even in Paris). On the fourth floor there was a retired advocate, Maitre Charles Duchamps, who had apparently been a 'star of the bar' in his day but was now crippled with arthritis. Nick had once played him at chess and won, and seemed disappointed he had not been invited for a return match. The Maitre was on holiday in the Vendée. On the same floor was someone of whom Nick was obviously in awe, a single lady of a certain age who worked as a weather presenter on television. "We've missed Myriam's broadcasts tonight but if you watch the channel for her *metéo* spot tomorrow you'll see her. She wears a different outfit every night. I'll bet her second bedroom is one big walk-in wardrobe." From the way he talked Nick would not be averse to walking into Myriam's wardrobe himself.

Chapter 4

Monday, my first day at the University and my first teaching day, went smoothly. I didn't take Nick's advice to hire a bike. Since I felt it was too far to walk, I took the metro. The Dean introduced me to some of the lecturers who shared the same corridor but who showed little interest in the latest bird of passage or in the subject of my classes. In the afternoon I met my students, eight in number. They all seemed anxious to learn and were pleasant people from a range of ages and backgrounds. In fact the anxiety was more on my side, that I would be able to give them what they had paid for. Although I could speak fluent French some of my pronunciations, I had been told, sounded as if I came from the Languedoc. Blame my ex-wife. I tried to excuse this by saying I had perhaps immersed myself too much in Cathar history but of course they would have spoken Occitan, not French.

Classes were every second day and the eightsome were expected to reel off short essays which they would write on Tuesdays and Thursdays and these would be discussed by all of us the following day. That gave me two days off during the week and weekends. My only other duty was to deliver a short series of lectures at the end of my six week stint which I had already written. After that I intended to go to Canada on a climbing holiday in the Rockies before resuming my proper job as a lecturer in medieval history at my college in London.

On the way back to my apartment I bought an evening edition of *Le Monde*. The front page headline immediately grabbed my attention. It translated as "Turin Shroud Stolen" and described that the holy cloth I had seen only two days ago, had been snatched that very morning as it was transferred from the Cathedral back its own adjoining chapel. The bold thieves had apparently made use of the fact that the Ducal palace was also joined to the Cathedral. The chest containing the Shroud had just been taken into the chapel when a smoke bomb exploded in the Cathedral. Those guarding the Shroud had rushed back to investigate and the thieves had locked the connecting door behind them. They exited with the Shroud chest through the door into the Ducal palace and loaded the chest into a waiting van which drove off. The white van had been stolen last week and fitted with false number plates. It was later found burnt out on the outskirts of the city near the motorway which leads to Milan in the east and the tunnel through the Alps to the west. There was no sign of the chest which had presumably been transferred to another vehicle. Nor was there any indication which way the thieves had gone or what form of transport they might have used to escape.

Three men wearing masks had carried out the heist. They had hand guns which they had used to knock unconscious two guards in the Ducal palace. The guards were then gagged and tied up while the thieves waited hidden in the Chapel until the Shroud chest was carried in by the team charged with transporting it the short distance from the Cathedral. The smoke bomb in the Cathedral had been a clever move to divert the men who had carried the chest into the Chapel back into the Cathedral and out of the way without the need to fire any weapons.

The whole operation was slick, ruthless and clearly the work of experienced criminals. But why had they done it? The Shroud was hardly something you could put on eBay or sell at an auction house. Were they religious extremists bent on destroying a sacred relic of another faith, jihadists targeting one of Christianity's icons? Or even ultra-protestants who saw themselves as modern iconoclasts destroying an idolatrous artefact? There was also perhaps a more mundane motive, an attempt to extort a ransom from the Catholic church. So far no group had claimed responsibility for the kidnap, if that was what it was. If the purpose had been to destroy the Shroud this could surely have been achieved by pouring acid over it or setting it on fire.

The inside of my newspaper carried a hastily composed article entitled "Curse of the Shroud" using archive material. It made much of the fact that fire had nearly destroyed the Shroud in Chambery in 1453, and again in 1997 when an electrical fault had sparked a fire in the Chapel while it was undergoing a restoration. It went on to describe how the cloth had become a source of dispute not only among scientists but within the Catholic church. In the front page piece the Bishop of Turin was quoted as saying that whoever had committed the crime was offending the faith of millions and that if they returned it, he was sure they would be forgiven by the Church. Not by the Turin tourism authorities, I mused, who were taking a dim view of one of the jewels in their tourism crown being pinched. Well, it was possible I might be one of the last people to set eyes of the famous cloth. Sceptical as I was about its authenticity, I would be sorry to see it disappear. Not because that would put an end to my role as a pundit, but because it acted as a useful focus for a debate about sacred objects and how they should be regarded.

That evening at 8pm I turned on the main television news to see if the robbers had been sighted or even caught. There was nothing on TF1 which tends to ignore stories outside the borders of the Hexagon. I switched over to France 2 and caught the tail end of a report from Turin. The President of the Society of the Shroud was lamenting the loss and making a plea for the Shroud's return. I tried France 3 and found myself face to face with my upstairs neighbour Myriam. It was *Metéo* time. The famed wardrobe had supplied a black silky trouser suit and red leather belt. I now understood why Nick was a fan. Myriam was stunning, with long black hair tumbling over her shoulders, ruby red lipstick around her flashing white teeth and lustrous brown eyes. In coming to this assessment, I totally missed finding out what the weather had in store for the next day. Maybe she would give me a personal forecast if I ran into her in the elevator.

The next morning I had no class as my seminar students would be writing their essays to be discussed the next day. Google maps told me it would take less than half an hour to cycle to the Sorbonne via Boulevard Sebastopol. Time for a trial run to see if I could still ride a bike. Until I was sure I would not be run over by the notoriously aggressive Paris drivers, I held off signing up to Velib and went in search of the bike left behind by the previous occupants of my flat.

The stair down to the cellars was behind the elevator, at the foot of the wooden stair used by Nick and Co. At the bottom I was standing on a narrow corridor of bare soil. Eight wooden doors with faded flat numbers stenciled on them, stretched along the wall facing me. Each door led into a concrete bay about two metres square and the same height.

I used the key which had been hanging in my kitchen to open the storage box marked 2/1 and switched on the light bulb hanging by an ancient flex from the ceiling. The bike was covered in spiders' webs and dust but looked as if it would clean up nicely. The tyres were soft but thankfully there was a hand pump on the crossbar.

I was reversing the bike out when a steel door at the end of the earth corridor opened inwards toward me and a man stood framed in the door. Coincidence had rung its bell. I was face to face with Hook Nose, the man from the Cathedral in Turin. It was definitely him. The slit eyes fixed on me but he said nothing.

I hope my shock and surprise did not show too much in my face. I felt I had to say something to justify my presence. He was the intruder but the intensity of his hostile gaze made me feel nervous, even threatened.

"Bonjour. I'm a new occupant," I burbled.

Without saying a word, he turned and pulled the steel door shut putting himself on the other side. I heard bolts being drawn across. Charming. But why was he here in the cellars of my apartment block? Was he carrying out some kind of maintenance work? He clearly did not remember seeing me in Turin. As I reflected on the coincidence of encountering him again, an ugly and fantastic idea entered my mind. No, it was too ridiculous. I had read too many detective novels.

Putting the incident out of my mind, I turned to the task of cleaning the bike. I got it up to the entrance hall and was about to put it in the elevator when a shrill voice came from behind me, speaking in French.

"Monsieur! What are you doing? It is strictly forbidden to take bicycles into the lift. Who are you anyway and what right do you have to be in this apartment block?" The speaker was a small white haired lady with sharp blue eyes and thin lips. Her skin was pale yellow and she carried a walking stick with which I was sure she was about to beat me if I did not give the proper answers to her questions.

Unaccustomed to such aggression and rudeness in

someone of her age (which I estimated was not less than eighty), I replied crisply, "Madame Adam, I presume? I am your new neighbour. In the flat beneath yours."

"You are nothing of the sort. You are NOT my neighbour. You are a tenant and I am a proprietor. I told that American he would face eviction if he dared bring his bicycle upstairs or leave it in the vestibule. And I told that 'Charity' which owns the flat that I would bring an official complaint if he did it again." She managed to pronounce the word 'charity' as if it was something immoral or illegal. "Do I make myself clear?"

"Perfectly," I replied.

"Now stand aside and allow me to use the lift. And keep that dirty bicycle away from me!"

She entered the lift, slammed the iron grille and ascended on high. I laughed out loud before it occurred to me that she had probably heard me and it would make matters worse. I had got off to a bad start in my Parisian home and I thought I had better make my excuses to Maria the concierge.

Chapter 5

Before I could knock at her door to tell her what had happened, Maria opened it and I realised that she had probably overheard every word of the altercation.

"Please come in," she said quickly. "Bring the bike out to the small garden at the back and you can clean it there." I did as she asked. "It's true, Monsieur Quillan, that bikes are not allowed in the lift or the landings, but you are new and you did not know. I should have explained that. Please, will you sit down? Will you take coffee with me?"

"With pleasure." I welcomed the chance to put matters right and also to find out why the man with the hook nose had appeared through the steel door. I began by explaining that I had met Nick and he had told me about the bicycle belonging to the Mackinleys. I went on to say that I had also met my neighbour across the landing.

"Ah yes, Madame Lafont. She is so crippled but she manages to do so much on her own. Her son comes from Normandy sometimes at weekends and brings groceries that are too heavy for her to get herself, but she is very independent. She has lived here for sixty years. She and her husband moved here shortly after their marriage. He died ten years ago. She really needs to move to more suitable accommodation but this area, she loves it so much. She once said to me that she wants to die here."

I nodded sympathetically and sipped my coffee. "And Madame Adam? Has she been here long?"

Maria's eyes filled suddenly with tears. "Yes, she has. She is always making complaints to the Association of Proprietors and..." Her voice broke. "She wants them to terminate my contract. She says that I am lazy and that I do not clean the common areas properly. One day there was a mistake with the post. I usually take the letters round the flats. Unlike many other blocks, we do not have mailboxes in the entrance. She was against spending money on them. Well, one day I put a letter for her into Maitre Duchamps' flat and he was away in the Vendée, and the letter stayed there for a week. She was very angry. I apologised but she said I had done it on purpose. My husband said he was going to go up and sort her out but that would have made matters worse. He said I was silly to take abuse from her. Now he is...not here so often..." Her voice tailed off and the tears ran down her cheeks. "I know he lives now with someone else and this is my only home and ....my job ... I am sorry Monsieur, I should not be telling you all this." She dried her eyes.

I was tempted to get up and give her a hug. That is about my only level of skill as a counsellor, having made my own marital mistakes which I was ill-equipped to remedy. So I tried my best to be sympathetic and let her talk. Madame Adam apparently had only one ally in wanting to change concierge and that was Monsieur Dieudonné who favoured replacing the concierge with an electronic security system and an outside (cheaper) cleaning service. My landlord the Charity trustees, in addition to Maitre Duchamps, Madame Lafont and the Fischers (the young couple originally from Strasbourg) had all been supportive of Maria and favoured the status quo. Myriam the Meteo girl did not have a say as she was not a proprietor, simply the tenant of a rich sugar daddy who never attended the annual meeting of proprietors. The only other proprietors, the Couadiers from Gers were an elderly couple, who were in the process of selling their flat and would soon have no say in the matter.

"After they sell or if one of the other proprietors changes, then perhaps Madame Adam will get her way," Maria concluded pessimistically.

What could a short-term tenant like me offer as comfort except to mouth comforting clichés. I was tempted to suggest that if her marriage was cracking up and she was unhappy here perhaps she could start now looking for another post but I held back. That was not what she wanted to hear at this juncture and she was clearly looking for sympathy and support. I had only known the lady three days and did not want to get involved. I decided to change the subject and mention the steel door and Hook Nose.

"Please be assured, Maria, I will take this bicycle back to

the cellar when I have cleaned it. I will try it today and if I decide to use it, I will always keep it there." I said it like a solemn oath. Then added as casually as I could, "May I ask what is behind the steel door down there in the cellars?"

"Oh, that is the connecting door to Brocando, the antique business on the corner. They rent three of the cellars which are not used by the proprietors. They have so much stuff next door that they are always looking for extra storage. If you don't need it for your bike I am sure they would be interested in your cellar too. I could speak to them for you. Oh, of course that should be your landlord, the Charity, who would need to decide."

Suddenly I realised that sweet Maria might not be as innocent as she appeared. If some of the proprietors did not use their cellars at all, perhaps Brocando rented them direct from Maria. Would they know or would they care? It was done all the time with parking spaces which were sub-let by caretakers.

"Would that be the gentleman with the shaved head whom I saw down there this morning?" I asked innocently. It was easier to describe him that way. After all there are degrees of hookiness, and one person's hook might be another person's natural bend.

Maria blushed. I am certain it was a blush. Was it because Hooky was doing a deal with her behind the proprietors' backs? Or was he showing attention to a lady whose marriage was on the rocks? Her answer gave no clue as to which it was. Or maybe it was both.

"Graziano is his name. He's from Bari in Italy. He has two partners but they work mostly at the big workshop and showroom in the Latin Quarter. Near to the old Roman Wall and your university. They come and go in their van and when it's open the shop next door is staffed by Zizi, a lady assistant. You should have a look there sometime if you want extra things for your flat."

It was time to take my leave. I now had a name for Hooky and I knew what he was doing down there. The newspapers continued to speculate on the motive of the robbers who stole the Shroud. There were apparently few clues apart from the CCTV of the van leaving the Ducal palace, since the thieves were all masked. They had hidden in the palace behind a connecting door and timed their move for the moment when the chest containing the Shroud was being moved and the church and chapel were sealed from the public. Was I being ridiculous by thinking these men from Brocando might have something to do with the theft in Turin?

That night I found a news documentary on television about the theft and was amused to see a clip of the panel discussion in which I took part. There was a lot of archive footage about the tests which had been done on the Shroud. The programme aired various theories as to why it might have been taken but there was still no sign of it. Nor any ransom demand.

It was a stuffy summer evening and I opened one of the windows in the lounge to let some air into the flat. The clock showed that it was approaching midnight. The side streets around the flat had quietened down. On the street below a large white removal van was double parked on the corner, backed up towards the door of Brocando. Graziano and his mates were working late. I put my head out to watch. Voices drifted up and I heard the words that sounded like 'van' something. They were shouted from one man inside the van to another on the pavement. He repeated an instruction about the 'van' and it sounded this time like "cigarette".

Two men loaded several heavy articles covered in thick grey blankets into the van and drove off. Then, to my astonishment I saw Graziano come out of the antique shop, lock up and walk to the door of our apartments. He pushed the buttons to operate the entry code and came inside. Oh dear, I thought, my suspicions about Maria's blush were correct. She really does have a lover and little good will come of it.

I went to bed, managed to fall asleep and was wakened up later by the noise from the flat upstairs. It sounded as if someone was opening the front door of Madame Adam's flat and closing it again. I laughed to myself at the thought of the old witch coming back late from an evening in Pigalle. She had just missed Graziano coming in and if she had caught him with Maria then she would have the ammunition she needed to get her sacked.

At my age I rarely get through the night without one visit to the loo. My flat had only one bathroom and was separate from the WC. Built long before sophisticated extractor fans which run for a few minutes after you put out the light, ventilation to the small toilet consisted of a square window opening onto a ventilation shaft which ran right up inside the core of the building. At the foot of the shaft at ground floor level were the rubbish bins which needed to be put out by the concierge on the appointed collection day. I had not noticed these when I first arrived because the shaft was hidden behind the main stair curling around the elevator. On the opposite side of the elevator and stairs was the wooden stair up to the attic rooms and down to the cellar. By opening the window of the loo I was able to create a draught through the flat. I wondered how the McKinleys had coped without the air-con which would have been essential kit in their native USA. During the previous periods I had spent living in France I had learned how to manage shutters, windows and doors to keep the sun out and the air moving without having to burn electricity. When I popped my head through the window to check if there was any movement in the air, my face brushed against a rope dangling against the wall and descending the shaft. When I closed the window in the morning to go off to the Sorbonne, it wasn't there.

Chapter 6

The bike ride was not without a thrill or two. It did as promised take less than half an hour but when I arrived at the university, hot and sticky, having been verbally abused by a few drivers, all was not well with my soul or my body. I decided to leave the bike locked in a bike rack at the Sorbonne and take the metro back at the end of my classes. Before I got back on the bike I would get myself a helmet and find where I could shower at the university end of the journey. Or I would simply give up the plan and take the Metro like most people.

Maria was nowhere to be seen when I entered the apartment entrance. I had only been a few minutes in my flat when the buzzer sounded. Outside my door was Madame Lafont looking distraught.

"I heard you come in, Monsieur, and I wonder if you have seen the concierge. I've been trying to reach her and she is not answering her door."

"Do you have her phone number, Madame?"

"No. I don't even have a phone. I don't need one." These two statements astonished me. The increasing insistence that everyone should fill in forms and pay official demands online had clearly not caught up with Mme Lafont. No doubt she went in person to pay her bills or perhaps she had yielded to modernity by setting up direct debits, or her son had done it for her. The second statement that she did not need a phone was daft since she obviously did need one now. And how would she tell her son in Normandy if she was ill and had to go to hospital or call an ambulance? I spared her the lecture on the need to have a phone these days, as she was so obviously upset about something.

"What is the matter, madame? Is something wrong?"

"Well, it's Madame Adam. I know she criticised you about the bicycle in the lobby but her bark is often worse than her bite. You see, she and I have known each other for nearly fifty years and although we don't always agree about things, we take coffee together on a Wednesday morning every week. She is quite lonely, you know, beneath that fierce exterior."

I thought there are more ways than one to become lonely and among them is to be nasty to everyone you meet for the first time. Thought it, but didn't say it.

"How can I help?"

"Well perhaps you can find the concierge. I shall start with her. Mind you, Félice (that's Mme Adam) will not be too happy to involve that girl. But I can't see what I can do otherwise. I have to look into her flat to see if she's alright. You see we always have coffee at eleven o'clock on Wednesday. Did I say that already? We take it in turns and today it was to be in her flat. I went up on the dot. You see she doesn't like it if you're late. Only there was no answer and I know she would never go out without telling me. She has good health for her age. In fact she's younger than me and never stops telling me how she has never had a day's illness in her life. Of course that doesn't stop you getting something awful like an aneurysm. But if she had fallen she would have called the ambulance. She does have a phone."

I decided not to say I thought I had heard someone entering her flat in the middle of the night as I might have been mistaken or perhaps it had been the Fischers on the same landing returning late, but I was sure the noises had come from above me.

"Please allow me to call the concierge," I offered. "I have her mobile number." I took out my phone and dialed Maria. She answered on the first ring.

"Allo, who is this?"

"It's me, Max Quillan from the second floor. I have Madame Lafont with me and she's worried that Madame Adam has been taken ill. She had a rendezvous with her and no one is answering the door. Do you have a key."

"No," replied Maria sharply. "All the owners and tenants leave a spare key with me but she refused. I suppose you could call the *pompiers* but I won't do it. She makes enough trouble for me as it is and if she does not need help….well, it's me who will get the blame."

"I understand. Leave it with me and Madame Lafont, but it could be that someone will come to try to gain entry. I think you will need to get involved at that point. Where are you now, Maria?"

"I am in the garden but I will come back and watch the door." This was a more brittle Maria than the tearful woman of yesterday morning. Apartment life in Rue Marronnier was certainly not dull.

I put it to my neighbour that we should try once more to knock at the door of the Adam flat. If we still had no reply, we could call a locksmith or the *pompiers*.

"Is there no one else who might have a key?"

"Alas no," the old lady confirmed. "She was very careful about her security and she said people could always lose keys or they could be copied. I'm afraid that she didn't trust anyone. There was a daughter but they fell out and anyway she lives far away from Paris."

"Ah well, the *pompiers* it is. If they can't get through the door they can always climb up from my flat or abseil down from the roof. Do you know the number?"

"Of course. It's 18." She said it as if she was in the habit of calling the fire brigade on a routine basis.

The *pompiers* were prompt and very good at their job. It turned out that all Madame Adam's keys were in the door, but on the inside and it was double locked. The flats on the fourth floor above Madame Adam belonged to the weather girl and the advocate. The latter had not left a contact number. Myriam was uncontactable, no doubt divining tomorrow's weather at the television station so they got the lawyer's keys from Maria. A fireman abseiled down and went in through the french windows on the street side of the building. While we were waiting, Madame Lafont had offered me a glass of Muscat which we were sipping when the pompier came to the door.

"I'm afraid it's bad news. I understand she was a friend of yours, Madame?"

Madame Lafont nodded."Well, we've been neighbours for a long time." Not quite the same thing I mused.

"I'm sorry to tell you that she is in her flat but she is dead. I've called police and ambulance and they'll take it from there." With that he went on his way to his next crisis, leaving me to cope with the second tearful lady in two days.

"Can I call your son in Normandy? Would you like him to come through?" I suggested, but she was already stiffening with stoic resolve.

"No thank you. He is due on Saturday morning. I can wait until then. I'll take a sleeping pill and I will be able to talk to the police in the morning. I'm sure they will want to talk to those who knew her and of course I would like to find out what happened. I won't if I run off to Normandy."

They make them tough in the Paris bourgeoisie. I went down to see how Maria was taking the news. She was clearly shaken. As I stood at the door to her apartment the front door opened. I was hoping it might be Myriam the *Metéo*. In all the excitement I had missed what the famous wardrobe had provided to accompany tonight's weather forecast. What I did not know was that apparently on Wednesday nights she and her colleagues went out for dinner after the last bulletin.

Instead it was Monsieur Dieudonné who swept in the front door and went straight to the lift. He showed no interest in why an ambulance with blue lights flashing was parked outside the door. As the concierge was a non-person to him he would hardly have been likely to stop to chat but I suspect most people were non-persons as far as he was concerned. I made a silent bet that he worked in a job in which he could vent his disdain on others. Like a bank manager or public official. I had come across people like this before in France. Their role involved serving the public or their clientele but they saw it as having accorded them a status by which the public served them.

Maria was in a strange mood, her face pale and drawn. Not the vulnerable wounded bird of yesterday or the nervy lady of a few hours earlier who was unwilling to get involved. She asked me if the *pompiers* had said anything about how the old lady had died.

"Not a thing," I said. "No doubt we will learn more tomorrow." She seemed shocked and unwilling to talk further. As we stood together in the vestibule in an awkward silence, the police arrived so I left her and went up to my own flat.

Not much later the buzzer was sounded by an officer from the city police who was going round all the flats to explain why there had been a fire engine, then an ambulance and a police car outside, and asking if anyone had seen Madame Adam earlier.

The next day was Thursday - not one of my teaching days, so I decided to sleep late. My buzzer went again as I was making breakfast. This time it was a plain clothes policeman, an Inspector Marty, who wanted to know why I had become involved in calling the fire brigade.

I told him that I had arrived on Sunday and had only met Madame Adam once. I thought it wise to tell them about the spat over the bicycle and it turned out they already knew. My silver haired neighbour or Maria had obviously ratted on me.

"Where is the bicycle now, Monsieur?" I was annoyed by the question. What in hell did this bicycle have to do with a lady who died locked in her flat – from the inside. I told him I had left it at the Sorbonne but couldn't resist asking him a question.

"Do you normally investigate so thoroughly when old ladies collapse in the their flat with the door locked? Surely she died of natural causes and that's all there is to it."

The policeman gave no sign of annoyance at my question. "We'll know more after the autopsy, sir. Until then it's too early to know how she died."

He asked when I would be available to talk to his senior officer. I told him I would be at the Sorbonne during the day on Friday if needed but here all weekend.

No one bothered me during the seminar and I left the Sorbonne at five o'clock on Friday to brave the traffic, clutching my brand new cycling helmet. On arrival in Rue Marronnier I obediently took the bike down to the cellars. Madame Adam would be looking on with approval, more likely from below than above. No sound could be heard from the steel door but as I pushed the bike towards my 'cage' marked 2/1, I stepped in what looked like an oil spill in front of the door 3/1. Against the dark earth of the floor I assumed that was what it was. It wasn't. When I got upstairs from the cellar I could see exactly what it was. Sticky, brown-red blood.

Chapter 7

A host of thoughts ran through my head. There had been a sudden death in our apartment block. Albeit that the deceased was found upstairs in her locked flat perhaps she had been wounded down here and stumbled upstairs and bled to death. Not before double locking the door behind her. That was not plausible. It was more likely that the blood was hers, and lots of it was right outside my cellar the day after we had an altercation. Worst of all, my sport shoe had stepped in it and left a footprint. Indeed not one footprint but all the way up the stairs from the cellar were imprints of my sport shoe. This was not funny. If I feigned ignorance, when they would eventually search in the cellar I would look so, so guilty. They would ask why I did not mention it. If I drew their attention to the blood it would look as if I were trying to explain away the incriminating footprints in a clever attempt to head off suspicion. And if I washed off the shoe and the prints, I would look utterly guilty for tampering with evidence. This was all going to hell on an electric bike.

I decided that I must tell the police about the blood before they found it themselves. That meant getting in touch with

Inspector Marty, the officer who had interviewed me the previous day. Fortunately he had given me his card with his number. I called it and said I had discovered some blood in the cellar and it might be relevant to their enquiry. I admitted I had stepped in it by accident and would be happy to tell them more. He listened but it seemed to me there was a sceptical tone to his voice. Anxious to convince him I was innocent, I went further and suggested they might like to seal off the cellars in case someone else disturbed the blood. That was a mistake. No professional likes to be told how to do their job. However, within the hour the blue lights of a police car had pulled up outside. The cellar was sealed. Marty took my shoes and told me not to leave my flat until Commissaire Janvier of the *Police Judiciare* called on me in the morning.

Those familiar with the Maigret detective novels of Georges Simenon which appeared between 1931 and 1976 will know that Chief Inspector (Commissaire) Maigret had four trusty lieutenants: Sergeant (Brigadier) Lucas, and Inspectors Janvier, LaPointe and Torrence. Depending on which version you prefer, Torrence left to run a private detective agency ("O") or was killed in an earlier book. Janvier was the one with whom Maigret used "tu", the more personal form of address than 'vous'. He was Maigret's right hand man despite being written out of the BBC TV adaptations in the sixties in favour of an enlarged role for Lucas. Simenon said that Rupert Davies who played Maigret in that series was his ideal. I was interested to see how the real-life Janvier measured up to the characters I had learned to love from the books.

Needless to say I was not going to mention the famous detective in an attempt to make light of the meeting. In fact I was nervous in case I should be seen as a suspect in what was rapidly assuming the case of a suspicious death.

The Commissaire buzzed my door at nine exactly accompanied by a colleague he introduced as Sergeant Sorgesa. Janvier turned out to be a charming man but behind his friendly manner I sensed a sharp mind. He seemed to have read mine.

"Please relax, Docteur. You are not a suspect in anything," then added with a laugh, "At least not until we have a post mortem report."

"Thanks. I replied. "I will relax even more if you can call me Max. I am embarrassed that I stepped in that blood in the cellar and complicated matters. At least I assume it was blood?"

"We'll soon know. I am having it analysed this morning and compared with the dead lady's. You were right to advise us of the blood in the cellars. Why were you there?"

"I was putting away the bicycle that I found in the cellar belonging to my flat…."

"Ah yes, the bicycle about which you and Madame Adam had a little disagreement."

"It wasn't so much a disagreement as a misunderstanding. I did not know that bicycles were forbidden in the lift and she put me right."

"In no uncertain terms, I believe. As was her wont."

I was taken by surprise that he already knew of my exchange with the dead lady and that she was by nature an aggressive person. I thought of asking who had 'shopped' me but I was sure he would not say. To my relief he did not dwell on the bicycle incident.

"Yes, you are a new arrival and it was your first encounter with Madame Adam, I understand. Can you take me through the time line and explain what you are doing here and when you arrived."

I did. At one point I turned and saw that Sergeant Sorgesa was taking notes of our conversation sitting behind me out of sight near the door. He, like Janvier, was in plain clothes and from a different division to the city police who had turned up after the *pompiers* left. Janvier sat on the settee with the light of the street windows at his back. I was in an armchair facing him. Well, at least it was not an interview room at the police station.

"So, let me sum up what we know so far," he said when I had finished explaining my presence in Rue Marronnier. "You normally live in London and your ex-wife now lives in Beziers. You were allocated this flat by the Sorbonne while you were giving seminars about the Cathars in your capacity as a medieval historian. You had never been here before. You arrived late on Saturday from Turin where you had been viewing the Holy Shroud and you had never met Madame Adam previously. You thought you might use this bicycle. Who told you about it?"

I explained about Nick and suggested that he was a good

source of information, as well of course as Maria.

"We'll certainly be speaking to everyone in the building. Or at least those who were here between Sunday and Wednesday. I understand some of the occupants are away at the moment. Did you know that Madame Adam wanted to replace Maria as concierge?"

I was beginning to appreciate his interviewing style. He would share information with me or confirm certain things, then switch to a quick question to catch me off-guard. At least that was what it felt like.

"Yes, I did know. I went in to Maria's to apologise for the mistake with the bicycle and she told me about Madame Adam's scheme." I tried to explain that I was simply a tenant and knew very little of the politics of the apartments. Indeed I had not met any of the other occupants except the ones already mentioned.

"Thank you, Docteur Max for being so open with us. I'm afraid I will need to talk to you again tomorrow. Would late afternoon suit? Before I go is there anything else you need to tell us?" He raised one eyebrow as he said it.

"Well, there is something," I said. "During the night on Tuesday I heard a noise from the floor above which sounded very much like someone opening and locking the doors of a flat. I can't swear it was the one above but that's what it sounded like. But I doubt it was Madame coming in at that hour."

"What time was this?"

"About two in the morning. I got up for a pee."

"And did you see anyone else? Maybe someone in the street?"

"Well, earlier around midnight the people from the antique shop on the corner were loading their van. I assume they need to do it at funny hours to avoid blocking the traffic."

"And did you see their faces?"

"No, but one of them was the proprietor. The bald headed one with the hooked nose. I think he's called Graziano. He came into the building after the van left."

"Oh, and how do you know what he's called?"

"Maria told me his name. I believe he rents some cellars down in our building. Brocando have a connecting door. He opened it while I was fetching the bike. I assume he must know the code to our entrance. Maybe he was going to check they had closed the connecting door." Any suspicion that he had paid an after midnight visit to Maria was not for sharing.

Nor, I realised, had I disclosed my previous sighting of Graziano. Because I had not mentioned the noise in the night at first and Janvier had winkled it out of me, I was beginning to feel defensive, as if I was holding back some guilty secret. To tell him now that I had spotted Hook Nose in Turin would have seemed bizarre, so I didn't say anything. I had also forgotten to mention the rope in the ventilation shaft and before I had a chance to tell him about it, Janvier caught me off balance with another question.

"Before we go, may I ask you if we can take your fingerprints to compare with others in the cellars." he said it as if I did not have any choice so I obliged. "I am afraid that we will need to keep the *baskets* you were wearing last night when you stood in the blood. If that's what it proves to be. We need to compare it with the other samples. Won't keep them long."

I then realised that I would now be without my favourite sport shoes (which the French call *baskets*). I had kept my luggage to a minimum for this trip and would need to go shopping later to replace them.

The other policeman put away his fingerprint kit and they prepared to leave, reminding they would be back on Sunday afternoon. As they reached the door I pulled a reverse Colombo on him, hoping to catch him off guard.

"May I ask you something, Commissaire. You are from the *Police Judiciare*. Is it usual for you to look into the death of an old lady in her flat with the doors locked? Is there something suspicious about it that brings such police activity?"

He looked back at me with a Mona Lisa smile, turned away and closed the door behind him.

Chapter 8

I took the metro to La Defense, the futuristic clump of high rise buildings due west of the Champs Elysee. It was centered on a paved open area above which towered a huge central arch containing offices. Down in the basement level there was an Auchan where I would be able to get new sport shoes and a full range of groceries. Normally I would have enjoyed such a shopping trip but I had a growing sense of foreboding that I was caught up in something sinister.

The smiling Janvier seemed unthreatening at first but what if this was his trick, lulling people into a false sense of security and then hauling them down to the police station and making them confess. Of course, I had nothing to confess except perhaps that I had not told him about the rope in the shaft. I decided I would tell him everything when he came back the next day, even about meeting Hooky in Turin, and run the risk he would think me a touch paranoid. Of course, as the old saying has it, just because you're paranoid doesn't mean they are not out to get you.

In the supermarket I was shocked at the prices of food

compared with the UK but I got a bargain with a pair of sport shoes on sale and got back to Rue Marronnier just after lunch. Maria was cleaning the vestibule and looking depressed. Despite this she greeted me with a smile and to my surprise offered to help me upstairs with my groceries. Sensing this would be a chance to learn more from her about the drama which had unfolded in the past week, I accepted. When she brought one of the heavy bags into the kitchen, I invited her to sit for a moment.

"Maria, do you think there is something suspicious about Madame Adam's death? The police seem to think so."

"I don't know, Max. Can I call you Max? You asked me to." She looked as if she might burst into tears again. "If the police think that someone killed Madame Adam, then they will think it was me. She hated me and she wanted to get rid of me. Perhaps they will think I killed her to keep my job. But how could I have killed her? She was locked in her flat. No one could get in. I don't understand what is going on. Now another set of police have come and they have closed off the cellars. They say it is a crime scene. How can it be a crime scene? Madame Adam was found in her room."

"Then you have nothing to worry about," I consoled.

"But I do. You see some of the proprietors never use their cellars. They gave me the keys. Graziano from Brocando next door asked me if he could have some for storage. He paid me. I said I did not want money but he insisted it was gratitude. But he doesn't come upstairs. They have their own door and bring things in and out that way. The thing is I have no right to this money but I need it and maybe they will accuse me of this crime."

So I was right, she was sub-letting. "Did you tell the police about Graziano using the cellars?"

"Yes, I told them but I did not say that he gave me money. If they find out then will they accuse me of this crime?"

"What crime, Maria? No one has said Madame Adam's death was other than an accident or maybe a heart attack. We don't know. The police have not said anything. As for the cellars, if the proprietors gave you the keys and said they were not using the cellars, as concierge you had the right to allow Brocando to use them. That was no crime."

She looked slightly relieved, but apparently there was more.

"No, but I did something else that may get me into trouble." She paused and I waited. "You see, Monsieur - I mean Max, Graziano asked me to do something else..."

"You don't have to tell me if it is personal."

"Oh no, it's not like that. My husband is not here now but I would not do that. I am a Catholic and I go to mass. It was more a favour he asked and said he would pay me just to look into some of the flats when the owners were away. Some of the people who live here are quite wealthy and they have beautiful furniture in their flats. Unlike yours, Max." She smiled, relieved to be confessing even if I was far from a priest. "Graziano said these antiques could be valuable and he could sell them for the owners."

"He wasn't intending to steal them was he?"

"Oh no. He said he only wanted to see what was there. If he had gone to the door and asked to look at their furniture I doubt if any of the owners would have let him in. When he was in the flat if he saw something good he told me he would come back and say to the owner that he had heard from a friend that they had something they might want to sell. That way he would not waste time getting doors shut in his face." Maria's naivety in swallowing this yarn was breathtaking.

"Did he do this often?"

"Only once so far. It was last week. Maitre Duchamps has a very nice flat with a lot of very nice things. He is quite old and if he sells his flat there will be a lot of things of interest."

"How did he know Maitre Duchamps was planning to sell? Did you tell him?"

"No, he must have learned it from someone else. I only heard myself a few days ago from Madame Lafont. That's why I was worried if the Maitre sells his flat and someone buys it who sides with Monsieur Dieudonné and Madame Adam, I will be out of a job. I am telling you because I feel I can trust you."

"So he came here on Tuesday night and asked if he could borrow the keys to Duchamps' flat? Is that right?"

"Yes, It was Tuesday. Yes, it was. How did you know?" I didn't answer and she went on. "It was around midnight. Very late anyway. He said he was just back from Italy and gave me a bottle of perfume and a 100 euro note. It's not that he charmed me. In fact I don't really like him but he is a very forceful person. He said he would only be twenty minutes.

He had wakened me up and I wanted to get back to bed. So I told him to put the keys back in my box when he left and they were there in the morning. To tell the truth, I am a little afraid of him and I'm sorry that I ever gave him the keys to the cellars and the Maitre's flat. It's too late now and with the police probing into Madame Adam's death I am afraid I will be in trouble. What do you think I should do?"

I was now sure that Maria was not involved sexually with the sinister Graziano but I wanted to help her. In her emotionally fragile state she was liable to land herself in trouble with the police. Maybe I was flattered she had chosen to confide in me, but until Madame Adam's death was cleared up, I advised her to keep quiet meantime about the keys. That advice was to cause me agonies of regret in the days to come.

"By the way, Maria, did you mention to the police that Madame Adam had quarreled with me about the bicycle?"

"No, Max, I did not. I have a problem trusting policemen. My grandfather was tortured and killed by the Salazar regime in Portugal when my father was a boy. He brought me up to mistrust the police. So I will follow your advice and keep this to myself. I will not anger Graziano by stopping him from using the cellars but I will not be bullied or bribed into giving him any more keys. Sorry but I must go now and finish my cleaning. Thank you for listening."

She meant it as a compliment but I felt a little guilty for suspecting her of being involved with Hook Nose and teasing so much information out of her. I always was a bit too inquisitive, as my mother kept telling me. But I knew now that it was Madame Lafont my neighbour on the landing who had told the police about my spat with Madame Adam. I couldn't really blame her but it given me a motive, that is if there had been a crime. The other obvious suspect was poor Maria but even if the blood in the cellar turned out to be from the body in the locked flat, there remained the question of how the body got there. All of that supposed that her death was not natural. The next day I found out with certainty that it was not and the mystery deepened.

Chapter 9

Commissaire Janvier was alone when he came to my door the next day. The smile was still there but he seemed to be energised, and a lot more willing to tell me what was going on.

"First of all, Monsieur Quillan, I have to tell you that this is now a murder enquiry and thanks to you among other things we are able to be sure about that."

I sat up with a jolt. He saw the surprise on my face.

"First of all, we were suspicious when we examined the lady's body in the flat. At first sight it looked as if she had fallen and hit her head on the fireplace. But the wound did not correspond with where her head supposedly struck the edge of the fireplace. Second, there was not enough blood on the floor. She had bled out considerably and it was not until we found – or rather you found – the blood in the cellar that we knew where she was killed. The blood was a match and it was not possible that she had been wounded, whether by accident or by a blow, in the cellar and staggered upstairs, locked herself in and died. There would have been blood all over the stairs or elevator. Close forensic examination of both has not yielded any blood."

"Are you saying she was killed in the cellar, her body wrapped up and taken to her flat?"

"You've got it in one. A massive blow to the head. No weapon found. No fibres on the body so it must have been wrapped in a plastic sheet or bag."

"Do you know when she died?"

"That's not a secret. The pathologist puts it sometime on Tuesday evening." He smiled. "Of course you were here in your flat and you don't have an alibi." He saw the shock on my face and laughed. "But we never really saw you as a suspect anyway. Nor the concierge whose job was threatened by the deceased and who seems to be so frightened we will think she did the old lady in. For a start the pathologist confirms that whoever struck the fatal blow, it certainly was not a skinny young woman like Maria. There are plenty of people who might have wanted to see the back of Madame Adam whose hobby seems to have been scolding people, and we have talked to a few, including her daughter, but none had the opportunity or were anywhere near the cellars on Tuesday."

"You said she had a daughter. Estranged? I think Madame Lafont suggested that was the case." I quickly added.

"Yes, estranged is putting it mildly. Madame Adam actually a 'Mademoiselle'. She was a single mother who gave up her child for adoption and when the daughter traced her birth mother, hoping for a happy reunion, all she got was a torrent of abuse for having dared try to get into her mother's life. Poor woman was appalled. She didn't need any inheritance and is happily married to a successful businessman but her mother accused her of wanting her money. As you probably know, in France children have strong inheritance rights. Madame Adam was not wealthy but apparently had a good pension from the state as she was a civil servant in quite a high position."

No doubt being as popular with her colleagues and those who had the misfortune to need her co-operation, as she was in this apartment block. I was delighted that Janvier was being so open with me. Especially as I was no longer suspected of anything. It turned out that in exchange he wanted more information from me and I was happy to give it.

"Monsieur Quillan, Max, if I may. I want to ask you about two things which may well have a bearing on the crime. First is the noise of a door you heard being unlocked and locked on the floor above you after midnight on Tuesday."

"The more I think about it, the more sure I am it came from the dead lady's flat. Did you speak to the Fischers – I think that's their name – who live on that landing?"

"Yes, we did speak to them and they confirmed they heard someone closing a door somewhere in the building during the night but their bedroom is around the corner from the front door to the Adam flat. And they couldn't say what time it was. The time you gave us is more precise."

"It's a locked room mystery isn't it," I said brightly. "You have a body in a locked room. The exits are all locked from the inside. How was it done? I've read a few detective stories with that scenario. It seems to be - or was – a favourite sport in France. The first was 'Murders in the Rue Morgue'. Then 'The Yellow Room' by Gaston Leroux. I think there was even one of the Maigret stories like that but I can't remember which one."

"There were actually two by Simenon but the detective in both was not Maigret. The first 'The little house at the Croix-Rousse' came out before Maigret appeared when Simenon was writing in his original name of Georges Sim. I don't think it ever appeared in English translation, so you may not have read it."

Surprised that the policeman shared my appreciation of French detective fiction, I told him that when I was a student I used the Maigret books to improve my French as they had simple sentences and were generally short. He laughed.

"You must have acquired a strange vocabulary for a history student."

"What was the second locked room mystery by Simenon?" I asked, hoping to continue the interview in this atmosphere of detente.

"'The night of seven minutes'. It's in the collection 'The thirteen mysteries' and the detective is someone he calls G-7."

"Yes, I've read that book but had forgotten the story. You seem to have a very good knowledge of the Simenon *oeuvre*."

"Commissaire Janvier was my grandfather." He looked at

me with a straight face as he said it.

I could not tell if he was pulling my leg, so I teased him back. "My favourite locked room mystery is 'The Yellow Room' in which the detective turns out to be the murderer".

"And was solved by the journalist Rouletabille," he countered. "Maybe this one will be solved by a historian but I have a solid alibi." We both laughed.

"To be frank I am scratching my head on how this one was done," he went on. "The blow was struck in the cellars and the body brought up to her flat, presumably wrapped in a sheet. It was laid out to look as if she had fallen and hit her head but there was not much blood on the ground. The policeman who attended thought the death suspicious. He alerted *Police Judiciare* and they sent me. At that point, until you told us, no one thought of looking in the cellars. Then the pathologist pointed out the wound was caused by an instrument like an axe and could not have come from the fireplace. It could have easily slipped by as an accidental death which of course it was made to look like. The murderer then double locked the door and exited. How? Where? The windows are already closed. We have checked for secret doors and trapdoors and there are none."

It was time to share my discovery. I hoped it would not spoil the mood.

"I'm no Rouletabille, Commissaire, but can I tell you something else that I saw that night which may or may not be of relevance? It may even suggest a solution."

"Certainly. You mean the Brocando van leaving about

midnight and the proprietor coming into the apartment entrance?"

"No. I did see that and I want to speak to you about that man, but this is something I didn't have the chance to mention when we talked yesterday." I put it that way to suggest it was his fault for not asking, rather than mine for being evasive. "When I got up for a pee in the middle of the night I opened the ventilation window in the small toilet to let some draught through. There was a rope hanging down outside my window coming from further up the shaft. I looked again in the morning and it was no longer there."

Janvier looked pensive and eventually said, "I see. Very interesting. What kind of rope was it?"

"The sort you use to tow a car or tie down a trailer cover. Thick. Dirty brown. It wasn't new and it wasn't nylon."

"Very good. We will examine the shaft for fibres to see where it was secured. What you are suggesting is that the murderer used the rope to escape from the locked flat through the bathroom window into the shaft, and then came back later and removed the rope."

"But the rope was not there in the morning of Wednesday and the body was not discovered until the early evening. How did the murderer get back into the flat to get the rope if it was double locked? Madame Adam would not give her keys to anyone so there was only one set and it was inside."

"Tell me more about this rope. Was it hanging from the flat above you – the old lady's - or from the top floor flats, both of which have windows in the toilets opening into the shaft?"

"I'm sorry I just don't know. It was dark in the shaft. I only noticed the rope because it brushed my face when I stuck my head through the window to see how much air was moving. It could have been from the top floor on either side."

"Well, I don't think it was Myriam Boudienne's flat. She was at home that night and unless she was an accomplice of the killer (I'm not serious by the way), she would have heard someone going out her toilet window."

Now was the opportunity for me to point Janvier toward Graziano's Tuesday night visit to the apartments.

"Then it must have been Maitre Duchamps' flat." I suggested. "I know he is away. Maria told me. But what if the killer got hold of keys and used them to enter the flat and secure the rope which he used to abseil down from the old lady's flat after locking the door and closing the window. By the way, the toilet windows in these flats open inwards and when they are closed the latch engages and you can't open them from outside without breaking the glass. You probably found the toilet window shut."

Janvier nodded. "We did. Yes, that makes sense. He then went back up to the Maitre's flat, untied his rope and took it away. I will send our forensics people up there to see if they can find any rope fibres. Now, about the man you saw in the cellar."

"Maria calls him Graziano and says he is from Bari. Apparently he owns the shop next door and another in the Latin Quarter which is bigger and has a workshop cum warehouse. He uses some of the cellars as extra storage. He came into the cellars when I was taking out the bike on Tuesday morning. The connecting door to Brocando is metal and the bolts are on the shop side. Well, actually he didn't come into the cellars. When he saw me and I said 'Bonjour', he turned on his heel and bolted the door shut without saying a word."

"Graziano, you say. Well that is one of his names. He is from Bari but he is Albanian. I can't say anything more but I can tell you that for us he is, as the expression goes, 'a person of interest'. It is one of the reasons that I was asked to oversee a possible crime in this building, adjoining his shop." I wasn't surprised to hear this but obviously Janvier was not going to say more. It was time for me to tell him about Turin.

"I have a confession to make, Commissaire," I began rather nervously. "I have seen this man before in Turin last weekend. He was in the queue to see the Turin Shroud ahead of me. He seemed to stand out. That's how I noticed him. His appearance, I mean. Then when he appeared through the steel door I recognised him. It was a huge coincidence meeting him again less than a week later. I didn't mention it because I thought you would think I had an over-active imagination."

Janvier frowned. The joshing about locked rooms was gone. "No, I don't think that. Did this man recognise you? Did you say anything to him about having seen him in Turin?"

"No. I don't think he recognised me. I was behind him in the queue. I was going to say 'what a coincidence' seeing you here but I didn't. I only said 'Bonjour'. His manner does not exactly encourage chit-chat."

"Indeed. I am going to offer you some advice, Max, which I hope you will take. Have nothing to do with this man and do not tell him you saw him in Turin. He is a dangerous person. As I said, at this point I can't say more than that, but I hope you will take my advice."

I was alarmed and probably it showed in my face. "What about Maria? Should she not avoid him as well? She has dealings with him over the cellars." I deliberately did not mentioned anything about Maria letting this guy have the key to Maitre Duchamps' apartment while he was away. I believed her when she said she had been bullied into it. Besides, he could have got the keys by borrowing them from the concierge's lodge.

"Leave it as it is for the moment. We are keeping an eye on this man and it is important that you stay away from him. Please do not tell Maria or anyone else that we have had this conversation."

"I'm sorry, Commissaire, but you've spooked me. I know you're not going to tell me why you are keeping an eye on him but can you at least say if you think there is a link between him and the theft of the Turin Shroud."

"You are a clever man, Max, and you have already helped me a lot but I must ask you to leave it there. As you say, I might get the idea you have too fertile an imagination."

"How did you get on with interviewing the other occupants," I ventured, hoping he would continue to share more information but he was clearly wanting to finish with me and test out the rope theory.

"I've talked to them all. Or at least the ones who were here on Tuesday night. Your friend Nick is quite a character. I will not be surprised if you and he try to solve this crime together but I strongly advise you and him to keep well away from it. Especially from the people at Brocando. Please don't think I am unappreciative of all the help you have given me so far but I must ask you not to discuss what you have told me with anyone else. OK?" With that he left me.

Chapter 10

My imagination went wild. Hook Nose had stolen the Turin Shroud with his gang of Albanians. He had brought it to Paris in his lorry and hidden it in one of the cellars in our apartment block so that if his premises were searched because he was a 'person of interest', nothing would be found. Presumably the old witch from the floor above me had stumbled on him in the cellars. I could just imagine the scene. She would have questioned him about what business he had to be in our property. Maybe his cellar door was open and she had spotted the chest containing the Shroud. Perhaps she unleashed a tirade 'as was her wont'. He realised that she would tell someone and he silenced her. His plan to make it look like an accident was a cool and clever way of shutting down any investigation into a murder.

He had acted quickly to get the body away from the cellars. If it been discovered there, questions would be asked about who had access. The old lady would have been carrying the keys to her flat when she came down to the cellar and getting her upstairs when no one was about would have been easy. He had his two helpers. She was frail and her body easily carried by men used to humping furniture around.

Even if he pulled off his locked room trick to make her death look accidental, he could not afford police nosing around the apartments. Above all he would need to find another hiding place for the Shroud chest. That had been the object under the blanket which I had seen loaded at midnight on Tuesday into the van. He had stayed behind to cover his tracks, locking the door from the inside and using the rope to escape. It all now made sense except for the basic question: why had he stolen the Shroud in the first place and what was he going to do now with something he could hardly sell on the open market.

It occurred to me that if I had gone to the cellar to collect the dusty bicycle after Hook Nose had come through the steel door, and I had spotted the chest in his cellar I would known instantly what it was. The blood on the earth floor might have been mine.

The only weakness in the killer's plan was that he had to rely on someone to give him the keys to the flat above Madame Adam to hang his escape rope. That person was Maria and she was easily bribed and bullied as he done previously with the cellars. But her fragile emotional state was something he would have noted. Was she too fearful to be able to hold her tongue under pressure from the police? Now that I had learned from her that his hold over Maria was not of a sexual nature or a form of loyalty, I began to worry that she was in danger. She did not know the police were looking at 'Graziano' or that the investigation now included the rope trick from the flat above the victim's. Despite Janvier's warning not to discuss what I knew with anyone, I had to find a way of alerting her to the danger she might be in. Tragically, I was too late.

When I knocked on the door of the concierge's tiny flat there was no answer. I tried her mobile. It was Sunday evening and perhaps she had gone somewhere for a meal or a visit. I invited Nick to join me for supper now that I had a full larder after my visit to La Defense. I vowed I would not divulge any of my conversation with Commissaire Janvier and I didn't. He asked me about the Sorbonne and I got a few more hilarious stories about life on the high-speed train network. I suggested to him there was scope for a humorous book on 'Memoirs of a train steward.' I said I was intending to have an *aperitif* party for my students and would invite him. Two of them were attractive girls in whom he might take an interest. Personally I was on sabbatical from relationships after an acrimonious and costly divorce.

I let Nick out the door in the kitchen and bolted it behind him. The evening had helped me take my mind off the ugly murder and the horrible suspicion that the Turin Shroud had found its way to Paris courtesy of Hooky. When I went into the toilet for a pee before going to bed, I saw through its open window a dark thin shadow moving in the ventilation shaft. It was a rope. The same type of rope I had seen there last Tuesday but this time tensioned by a weight it was supporting. I stumbled back from the window and let out a cry of horror.

At the end of the rope was a body, swinging gently to and fro against the walls of the ventilation shaft. I knew by the print dress she was wearing that it was Maria. He had killed her to prevent her talking and it was my fault. I had not warned her in time. I was consumed by grief, guilt and sorrow that this fragile young woman whose happiness had been snatched from her should have died in this way. It was a crude attempt to make her murder look like suicide. Not for a moment did I believe she had hung herself, even when the police who came in answer to my emergency call found what appeared to be a note in the side pocket of her dress. Later I learned it said 'I am sorry. I should not have done it.' They did not let me see what was written on it and I would not have known her handwriting anyway.

My grief gave way to anger, first against myself for failing to act, for suspecting that she might be involved with Graziano in some way, but most of all against the bastard who had done this to her. The very least I could do now would be to see that this was not treated as a suicide. The cunning and evil man who had tried to cover his murder of the old lady was now trying to pull another trick to blame Maria for his crime. When Janvier arrived I would make sure that he knew it. Perhaps I should have told him right away how the killer had got the key to the Maitre's flat by bullying and bribing a vulnerable Maria but that would have landed her in more trouble. It would have been a betrayal. Now I had to live with the guilt that I had done nothing, laughing and joking with Nick at supper while she swung at the end of a rope in the ventilation shaft. As soon as I had known about the danger she might be in, I should have rushed downstairs. I might have been able to warn her. The minute that Graziano knew that his locked room ploy had not worked and that the police would be in murder hunt mode, she was at risk. She was the weak link in the chain.

When Janvier eventually arrived, before I could speak he paced the room and said hoarsely, "I feel responsible for this. I told you to say nothing to her about Brocando. I even said to leave things as they are for now. Do you know why?" He turned towards me and there were actually tears in his eyes. "Because I was not sure whether Maria was acting with him as a willing accomplice and how much she knew about Brocando. I even thought she might have been his lover when her husband was away."

Ashamed that my own thoughts had initially run the same way, I swallowed, too choked to speak. We were both obviously bad judges of character but I tried to console myself that I had believed Maria when she revealed how she had become a victim of the bully next door. Suddenly suspicious of everyone and unsure that Janvier would treat her death as murder, I asked him bluntly, "You're not going to allow this to be seen as a suicide I hope?" I was relieved when he replied tersely.

"No way. The policeman who came in answer to your call flagged it as a possible suicide. I have an idiot as a boss who saw a way to draw a line over the old lady's murder and take the note at face value. She had enough anti-depressants and sleeping pills in her bedside cabinet to put down a horse if she had wanted to commit suicide without going up four floors, wriggling through a window and bungee jumping to be throttled at the end of a rope. No, this will not be treated as suicide. It was clearly meant to look that way. Whether she wrote the note under duress or it was forged we can look into it but whatever it was, I'm going to get the bastard." He turned abruptly from pacing my lounge. "Do you have a whisky?"

I poured us both a good three fingers and he sat down.

"I should have told you more about the man you saw in Turin but if any of it had leaked out the whole operation could have been prejudiced. You see we have been watching this gang for some time. Essentially there are three of them. The man you know as Graziano is the leader and the other two are also Albanians. Possibly relatives. Occasionally they bring in other people, Albanians or criminals they know in France and Italy to help them. They started as people smugglers but then they found a much better way of making money. They run three businesses, one legit and two criminal. Upfront is the import-export business for antiques between France and Italy sold in legit shops like the one next door, or at auction. Although they use it to launder money it's peanuts compared with the other two sides to the business. First is the theft of antiques in both countries. They target a wealthy homeowner or chateau or museum. When the owner is on holiday or the chateau is closed for the season, they move in and cherry-pick the antiques. Now here's the clever bit. They don't sell them in the country they pinch them from. They take a full van to Italy from France and come back with lorryload of Italian stuff. That way the owners don't recognise their own furniture when it turns up at an auction. They also have a large workshop here in the Latin Quarter and they alter some of the pieces so that they are not easily identified as stolen. It's clever stuff but it's not the real money maker."

"Drugs?"

"Yes, you've guessed it. Some of the stuff coming back in the van from Italy has drugs hidden in the furniture. A lot of these old desks and sideboards have little secret compartments built into them anyway. Or they construct new ones at their workshop. We think this gang then sell it on to bigger cartels. They miss out on big profits but the fact that it is controlled by only three people means their share in bigger. Two of them are brothers and the other is a cousin. The only other people involved are hired as either tradesmen or drivers. They may not even know what is carried in the lorry."

"And was he in Turin last week?"

"Yes, he was. We clocked him entering France at Modane. He sometimes stops for a break in Lyon but if you have three drivers you can reach Paris in less than nine hours and still be legal on the tachograph. That is his regular route. There are plenty of big houses with nice furniture in the Milan/Turin area and they have a workshop cum warehouse just outside Turin. If he took the Shroud on Monday and brought it to Paris he could have arrived here sometime during Monday night."

"Why haven't you arrested him before now? Maria might still be alive." He looked hurt at the question.

"Well, for a start we had no idea he might be linked to the Shroud theft. In fact that has still to be proved, despite your sighting which in a court of law is only circumstantial. Stealing the Shroud would be a huge departure from the stuff they normally buy and sell. The forensic people found marks on the earth floor in one of the cellars that could have come from the chest containing the Shroud but it could be from another object. We – I mean the PJ - have been working with Narcotics teams and Interpol, trying to build up a pattern of their activity and find out who they are selling to. My bosses want the whole network wiped up, not just the Albanians. So even now I have been told not to bring this guy in for questioning in case we spook his network."

"What?! He was renting cellars from Maria. He almost certainly got the key to the Maitre's flat from her. What are you waiting for?"

"Cool it, Max. I am just as upset as you are and yes, I do feel guilty. But I will only talk to him as someone who uses the cellars and see what he says. No heavy stuff yet. If he took the Shroud and had it in one of the cellars he has certainly moved it. If he recognised you from Turin when he opened the connecting door, he will have decided to move it. Even if he didn't know you had seen him in Turin, when the old lady saw him and he killed her, he will have been forced to move it. We will not find it in Rue Marronnier and we want to get the Shroud back too, not just arrest a drug trafficker."

"Wait a minute," I protested. "There is no evidence that he saw me as other than one of the flat occupants and backed off."

"What if he asked Maria who you were. The man who has just arrived from Turin? Poking around in the cellars. It's too much of a …"

"Coincidence," I finished for him. "OK, then why didn't he kill me and not Maria?"

"Because she could link him to the murder of the old lady. And who says you are not next on the list? That is why I am telling you all this. If he really did spot you in Turin then you are in real danger. Besides, when we arrest him (and notice I say when and not if) you are going to be a key witness for us. You can put him in the Turin Cathedral on the eve of the robbery and you can put him in the cellars where the blood was found."

I thought I could also tell any future trial that poor Maria had been persuaded to give him a key to the lawyer's flat on false pretences, and that she was afraid of him, but I'm not going there now. The poor woman deserves to be spared that before she is buried. The threat to myself was also beginning to sink in.

"So what do you suggest I do? I can hardly go into 'witness protection' or whatever you call it in France. I have classes to give for the next seven weeks. This flat is part of the fee and if I don't give the classes I lose the right to stay here. If I move out to a hotel he'll find me easily."

"Leave it with me. I have a plan that will enable you to stay here and give your lectures. But I need to run it past my boss. I will come back tomorrow morning and check with you. What time do you usually leave for the Sorbonne?"

"That depends. I won't use the bicycle as it's now part of the crime scene in the cellars. It takes too long to walk and I don't fancy getting pushed in front of metro train by you know who. Taxis are expensive."

"I will give you a lift tomorrow by car. Meanwhile lock both your doors and, he added with dark humour, "Maybe even the toilet window. I'll have men in the building all night."

Chapter 11

S o it proved. As I was finishing my breakfast Janvier stood there with another policeman.

"This is Inspector Lerolle. He and Inspector Marty will be taking turns to stay in Madam Adam's flat for the foreseeable future. People in the building will be told that he is her long-lost nephew who is sorting out her affairs with her lawyer. The real lawyer has been warned to stay away meantime. They will be your guards in the building and my look-outs. Additionally they will be watching Brocando and who comes and goes. The code has been changed on the entry system and the other occupants informed. Here is the code." He handed me a piece of paper. "On that you will find my mobile and those of Marty and Lerolle. Each day a police driver will be waiting round the corner at this time, out of sight of Brocando. Same place, same car for each day you need to go to the Sorbonne. He will pick you up when you finish. All these men are armed. You may be amused to know that one of my men is from Occitanie and interested in Cathar history. When he heard the subject of your lectures, he volunteered to sit in the class to keep an eye on you. Unfortunately I had to say no." Janvier had got back his sense of humour.

"Just as well," I riposted,"he might have fallen asleep on the job." Jolly laughs all round before I set off in Janvier's car. He pointed out the pick-up point for the daily taxi. As we progressed through the Paris traffic I fired some questions at him that had been keeping me awake the previous night.

"Has anyone been in touch with Maria's husband? They still are married, I take it?"

"Yes, and yes. He's Irish and his name is Finbar O'Mara. When he's not on the road, he lives with a woman in Braga, a Ukrainian refugee. It's on the route he usually takes from Lisbon to Lyon carrying salted fish. He and Maria met when she was working as a waitress in Lisbon. She is originally from the Douro valley. Her parents live in Porto and when we release her body it will be returned to them. At the time they got married O'Mara had a regular Paris route, hence she got a job here. We checked his whereabouts on the times of the deaths and he was not anywhere near Paris at the times concerned. But he is coming to Paris at our request this morning by train with the tachographs from his lorry."

"Does that mean you think he could have bumped off Madame Adam as a favour, to save his estranged wife's job? And why did you check him for Maria's death?"

"The answer is that we always check the husband. Especially as we both know that it was not suicide. That has still to be confirmed by the autopsy but there have been a number of cases in which strangulation has been disguised as suicide by hanging and we need to know if the hyoid bone was broken."

"Which would suggest she was strangled and then hanged?"

"Exactly." We passed the rest of journey in silence, still afflicted by our respective feelings of guilt. I had a funny feeling he was not telling me everything but why would he?

To escape into the thirteenth century for the day was a relief. My seminar group had turned in some good work except for an older man I suspected of being an Opus Dei member who argued the Cathars were subversives who got what was coming to them. I bought *Le Monde* on the way home and scanned it for news on the Shroud. There was plenty of speculation but no new developments. The Torino police conceded it had probably left the city the day it was stolen. Some self-appointed experts claimed it was possibly stolen for a rich but mad American (a role for which there would be several candidates) who wanted it for his personal ticket to heaven. Another theory was that the ransom demand would come when the thieves were sure they had got away with the heist itself. The jihadist theory was losing ground. If Islamist extremists had taken it they would probably have lost no time in claiming responsibility for the theft for its publicity value. Or publicly burned it to get even more notoriety. The same went for iconoclasts and extremists of other religious persuasions. Was it a stunt by Extinction Rebellion or some other campaigning group to gain attention for their cause? On and on the speculation went and no one seemed to have a solid link. Interpol had been alerted and I wondered if my sighting of the Brocando man in Torino on Saturday and in Paris on Tuesday would have been passed on and checked against CCTV images.

Back in Rue Marronnier courtesy of Janvier's free taxi, I took the elevator to the third floor and buzzed the flat above mine. Inspector Marty opened the door and looked surprised to see me. Or was it embarrassment? On a table in the salon behind him was an array of small screens and I could see that one contained an interior view of my flat. They had obviously entered it and bugged it while I was out.

"I guess I had better be careful about having ladies back to the flat or you'll have some nice *kompromat*," I told him with as much sarcasm as I could put in my voice. "I didn't realise you were using the KGB playbook."

"My apologies, Monsieur. Commissaire Janvier asked me to come down and tell you about the cameras as soon as you were back but you have beaten me to it by coming here. We put them in for your protection. Please come in and I will show you where the camera positions are so that if you want privacy you can avoid them."

I grunted assent and entered the flat. The chalk outline was still on the floor where Madame Adam's body had been arranged with its head resting on the corner of the marble fireplace. The killer had even got hold of a set of folding steps to make it look as if she had fallen from them. He would have got away with it if he had managed to clean the blood from the cellar and an autopsy had not been ordered. Perhaps he had not seen the blood in the dark down there. Or they had forgotten to clean it up in their hurry to get the chest out to their van without being seen.

I looked at the CCTV screens showing my lounge and kitchen. There were none in the bedroom or bathroom. Marty pointed out that there was a motion sensor activated camera in the hall at the door and another in the cellars but as that was still sealed off, it was only a precaution. I tried to get more info out of him on the case. Had Maria's husband arrived from Lyon? Had the autopsy been performed on Maria? I didn't expect him to tell me the results but he had the perfect stonewall. He had been here all day setting up and didn't know anything. I gave up and went down to my flat to eat, and opened a nice bottle of Fitou I had bought in Auchan at La Defense.

It wasn't time for Myriam's meteo spot so I put on a Paris radio station. There was nothing in the news bulletin about the Shroud but my ears pricked up at another item. "*Police Judiciare in Paris have been investigating two deaths at a block of apartments in the ninth arrondissement. The first death was of a lady in her late seventies which occurred last Wednesday and the second death on Saturday which at first was thought to be a suicide, was of the concierge at the same block of apartments. Both deaths have now been classified as murders. Police declined to name the deceased but it is understood that a man arrived in Paris this morning from Lyon and has now been detained by police in connection with both deaths. Police have two days in which to question the man but refused to name him. A statement is expected in due course. Leading the investigation is Commissaire Patrick Janvier, known in police circles as 'PJ of the PJ'. He had no comment to make this evening. Now the crisis in food prices……"*

I switched off the radio and took a large swallow of wine. What the hell was going on? The man in custody was obviously Maria's husband, the Irishman. But why? Janvier had told me himself that he had an alibi for both murders. Unless this had broken down or his tachograph had shown something wrong, the man was nowhere near Paris when both women were killed. Obviously they would have to talk to him, but when there was a much more plausible suspect in the Albanian, why did they announce that he was being held. My imagination then started getting the better of me again. Lyon was on the route the Brocando van had taken from Torino. A lorry driver was an excellent job to have if you were moving furniture around, or drugs. What if Maria's husband was after all part of the gang and they had picked him up en route and brought him plus Shroud to Paris? The old Adam woman had surprised them loading the chest into the cellars and they killed her. Why did they risk putting the chest in our cellars and not in the Brocando premises? Well, 'Graziano' may have suspected that Janvier and his team were watching him and were liable to search Brocando. What better place to hide the chest than somewhere unconnected with the antique business (except by a bolted door few knew could open)? It made some sense to me. But why kill Maria? Did she know too much and was liable to crack if questioned about the keys to the lawyer's flat? They killed her to silence her. Her husband either was complicit or the Albanian killed her without telling him and made it look like suicide. Now that the Irishman had another woman in his life perhaps he was not likely to ask too many questions about her death. There was one other possibility. Horror of horrors, it was that Maria was actually part of the gang with her husband, or with the Albanian or with both, and filled with remorse and guilt, really had committed suicide.

Most of these questions buzzing around in my head were ill-founded and, as I found later, completely misguided. Sherlock had his 'two pipe problems'. This was a two whisky problem and I poured myself a second large one. The trouble was that while Sherlock woke up with the solution, I usually went to sleep and was none the wiser. I knew I had to speak again to Janvier. He knew what the autopsy had said. He had spoken to the Irishman and for some reason had put him in custody. Would he tell me anything or was I now in 'witness protection' to keep me out of his hair? Thinking of hair reminded me that once again I had missed Myriam's meteo spot.

As soon as I had showered the next morning I phoned Inspector Marty and asked if he could ask Commissaire

Janvier to call me when he had a moment. He would hardly pop out from questioning Maria's husband to make me a priority. It was a non-teaching day so I told him that I would mostly be at home reading and waiting for his call. I didn't tell him that I would be reading a detective novel to keep my mind away from real life murder.

It didn't work of course and Janvier didn't phone either. The fundamental key to all of this for me was whether or not it involved the Shroud. Never mind why it was stolen. If it was stolen by the Brocando gang all the facts fitted and they committed the two murders to cover their tracks. But if they did not steal it and the Albanian's presence in the queue last Saturday was only a coincidence, then the whole thing became two separate and unconnected crimes: the theft and the murders in Rue Marronnier. If that turned out to be true, then it did not matter if the Albanian had recognised or me not. In this case I no longer needed my watchdog.

The day crept by slowly. Nick knocked at the kitchen door again, I suspect to see if he could cadge his supper but I told him through the door I was sorry but I had essays to correct. It was a white lie since I would only see the essays the next day when I arrived at the Sorbonne, but I didn't want him to tempt me to disclose anything about the case and break my promise to Janvier. I hardly slept that night thinking about Maria and her husband, and why he had been arrested and not the Albanians. About three in the morning, despite Janvier's warning I was seized by a determination to have a discreet look at the other Brocando premises the next day.

In the morning I was going down in the lift when it stopped at the first floor and Dieudonné got in. I noticed that he had a short beard under his chin. With his shiny bald head, he looked as if his face was upside down. He was not a happy emoji. He looked away from me at the opposite wall of the elevator and spoke in a quiet passive-aggressive tone.

"You are the man who brought all the trouble to this place. We had a peaceful apartment block until you arrived. You are only a tenant. Why don't you find somewhere else to live."

We had arrived at the ground floor. He pulled open the flexible iron gate on the inside, pushed open the double swing doors behind it and let them spring back in my face.

"Thanks for the warm welcome," I wanted to say but he was already out of the front door which slammed behind him.

Chapter 12

The previous evening I was annoyed at Janvier for failing to call me. Now I was angry. I resented the fact that whether he liked it or not, I was involved in this affair and I deserved to know what was going on. I had never told him how to do his job but I had given him key facts to help him do it. My anger had spurred me to go on the internet and find out the address of the Brocando workshop and warehouse in the Latin Quarter. It was near to a section of Roman Wall that remained in Paris, just round the corner from the part of the Sorbonne where my classes were being held.

In the lunch break, I recruited Guiliano, the youngest of my students who, as his name suggested, was Italian, to help me with my plan. I explained that I had visited the shop and been told that the antiques on display were French whereas I believed they had come from Italy. I didn't want to go back in myself or they would think I was investigating them and being too nosey. Could he perhaps do some investigations for me without leaving names or contact details?

I had been well warned by Janvier not to go into the lion's den in Rue Marronnier and I did not intend to be seen here either, so I wandered round the corner from the premises and watched while my student went off on his mission. The building was probably a former warehouse or workshop. It had a large sliding door painted battleship grey which hung on metal wheels from an iron rail. This door was wide enough and high enough for a large vehicle to pass through and was fitted with a series of locking bolts to keep it secure when closed. At that moment it stood fully open and a lorry was parked in the street outside with the ramp at the rear folded down as if it was ready to be loaded up. This was the same vehicle used by the Brocando gang outside my flat on Tuesday night. It could be described as both a small furniture van or a lorry, adaptable to carry furniture around the city but powerful enough to make long journeys to Italy and back. From my vantage point I could see into the loading bay it would occupy when it was garaged inside the building. A curtain made of strips of thick plastic divided the bay from a larger space far in the interior in which a variety of furniture was stacked. To the side of the grey door was a brightly painted shop frontage whose windows were covered by a metal security grille. Through it I could see various expensive looking antiques on display. Guiliano went into the shop while I waited out of sight.

I moved to the corner of the street so that my line of sight was up the ramp into the interior of the lorry. It was empty but there was something about the space that gave me an idea.

"You were right, I think," Guiliano announced when he came back. "The furniture looks Italian to me but the woman told me it came from a chateau in the Loire. Don't take my opinion. I'm no expert. Does it matter?"

"No. I was just curious what they would say. Can I ask you to do one more thing for me? Do you see that lorry? Can you pace out the distance from the back of the lorry to the back of the cab. Then run up the ramp and pace the distance from the back of the lorry to the back wall of the cab inside. It'll just take a few seconds. I'll keep a look out."

He looked at me as if I had gone crazy but he did as I asked. It took him twenty seconds. To my relief no one appeared. Thankfully everyone seemed to be at lunch except for a woman in the shop. Perhaps this was the Zizi whom Maria had mentioned, transferred here from the Rue Marronnier shop now that it was closed. All the more reason to stay out of sight in case she had seen me coming and going from the apartment block.

"Sei e cinque," he said when he came back. "Sorry, six and five metres. Is that what you wanted to know? It obviously has a false wall behind the cab. In Italian we call it a 'vano segreto'."

I looked at him. "Guiliano, what did you say? In Italian I mean. Please repeat it slowly."

Now he really thought I was mad.

"Vano segreto," he repeated hesitantly.

"And if I said to you quickly the words 'van cigarette' would that sound a bit like 'vano segreto'?"

"Yes, but Italians usually pronounce Italian better than that," he said with pride in his language.

But Albanians don't, I thought. "What if it was an Albanian saying it?"

He laughed. "Now I see what you're getting at. This is about Albanians using this lorry with it's secret compartment to do something illegal. Maybe with smuggling cigarettes? No, it's drugs isn't it? That's why you want to know. But why you? Are you working with police?"

"Sort of," I lied. "I need to pass this information to them. It was an idea I had when I saw the lorry. Brocando have a shop beneath my apartment block. But can I please ask you to keep this to yourself. I am very grateful but it must stay between us. The police don't know about this yet."

He said he would and I offered to buy him lunch next week as a small token of thanks. He asked if we could go to an Italian restaurant. He was obviously missing Mama's cooking.

I bought us sandwiches on our way back to the classroom where the others were waiting. I felt the need to say to the others that I needed his help with translating something from Italian. Older man going off at lunchtime with handsome young student. Not good for the image in the era of sexual predators. I really was getting paranoid.

The taxi supplied by Janvier was outside when we finished at four o'clock but of the Commissaire himself there was still no sign when I checked my phone messages. I thought of asking the driver to take me to the *Police Judiciare* and try to pin him down there but it was Friday, the traffic was slow moving, and both the driver and I were hot and tired. So I went back to Rue Marronnier. I turned over in my mind what I should do about the secret compartment in the lorry. If I told Janvier how I found out he would know I had ignored his strictures to stay away from both Brocando premises, even if I told him I had sent my spy while I watched from a distance. I did not fancy a lecture from him, but I knew the police had to be informed. The 'vano segreto' was probably the way the thieves had brought the Shroud chest to Paris, with other pieces of furniture to make up a load. They had hidden it in the cellars of my apartment block where it was unlikely to be looked for. But where was it now? After the attempt to disguise Madame Adam's death as an accident had failed they clearly had to get it out of the cellars, which they had done on Tuesday night. Perhaps they had taken the risk of transferring it to the other Brocando premises. Not my problem of course, and not my business as Janvier was certain to tell me but I knew I had to tell him about the secret compartment. Perhaps an anonymous tip-off?

The idea of proving that Hooky the Albanian is the prime villain in all of this was not something I was going to give up easily. My thoughts kept going back to Maria and her husband. I knew now that her death was not being put down to suicide. The autopsy must have proved that or the radio news bulletin would not have talked about two murders. What of the husband? Was he part of the gang or not? Or was he a jealous thug who had struck down the old lady and murdered his estranged wife? Why else was he under arrest? Questions, questions and no way of getting answers until Janvier re-appeared.

Just as I sat down to eat my supper the door buzzer sounded. I rose from the table and opened the door. A tall, clean-shaven man with tousled red hair and broad shoulders stood there. Behind him stood Janvier.

"Doctor Quillan I presume,?" said the redhead. He pronounced my name as 'Kwill-an' in an accent that was unmistakably from the south of Ireland.

"May I come in? I'm Maria's husband Finbar O'Mara."

I stood aside and the two men came past me into the flat. I settled them in the lounge and popped my supper in the microwave for later. This was too opportune to miss.

"Beer, scotch or wine, gentlemen?" I offered. They each took a glass of Sauvignon Blanc from Gascony, my favourite white. I sat down and awaited an explanation for the visit. O' Mara was not wearing handcuffs and by his cheery manner did not give the impression of being under arrest. Far from it.

"I wanted to come and thank you for what you tried to do for Maria," he said. I was dumbstruck. What had Janvier told him? Both he and I knew we had not done enough to save her. Moreover, what were they both doing here?

"I wish it had been more," I replied. "But forgive me, I thought you were under arrest. Perhaps the Commissaire can start by explaining what I heard on the radio yesterday evening. I've been trying to reach him for two days." I looked at Janvier accusingly.

"I know," Janvier admitted. "Inspector Marty told me. There were reasons why I did not return your call. I will explain it all now and I hope you will understand."

"Please do."

"Well, I did tell you that Monsieur O'Mara was coming to Paris by train. Voluntarily. He satisfied us that he could not possibly have been here at the time of the murders. He has also satisfied us that he has never met any of the Brocando people. None of the times match up and we have his tachograph and our CCTV to prove it. He never featured in any of the surveillance and he has not been in Paris for several months. The Albanians passed round Lyon on their way from Turin but went nowhere near the apartment he rents there for overnight stays. We have confirmed the CCTV of the lorry route from Turin. It took them ten hours and they did it direct with only toilet stops."

"I'm sorry but I'm confused by all of this. It seems that Finbar here is innocent so why did you let the radio station know that you had a man in custody?"

"Actually it was my idea," put in O'Mara. "I knew about the Brocando man and I am pretty sure he did both murders. I gather you do too and I think I have convinced the police."

Like many men from the south of Ireland he often pronounced 'th' as 't'. This increased when he got more animated. His heavy accent reminded me of someone I knew from Cork but then again it could have been Limerick. I'm no expert.

Finbar went on, "You see Maria used to write emails to me even after we separated and I replied to them all. I showed them all to the Inspector here. I felt really guilty about leaving her here in Paris but there was not much I could do. My regular route had changed…."

He paused. Remorse was written all over his face. Commissaire Janvier accepted his demotion to Inspector and remained silent.

I said quietly through gritted teeth "We all felt guilty" and O'Mara resumed his story.

"I knew Maria was very unhappy here as concierge. First there was that old bitch on the third floor who was trying to get her sacked. Then that Albanian guy who calls himself Graziano turned up and asked to rent some cellars. The connecting door was already there but never used. She thought she was doing a good turn and he gave her money as a thank you. Then he used it to blackmail her. That was what it was. He would tell the old bitch that she had a wee number going unless she did as he wanted. That's how he must have got the keys to put that rope in the shaft."

He looked genuinely upset and ran his fingers through his curly red mop of hair. Now that he begun his story he clearly wanted to say more. "Maria was a waitress in a bar in Lisbon I used to go into a lot for the Fado music. We married in a hurry and soon found out we were chalk and cheese. At that time my route took me to Paris and she got this job. Sure, she was lonely. She was sensitive and emotional. You might say neurotic if you want to be unkind. I'm the strong silent type and she needed a lot of reassurance and I wasn't around to give it. I was away a lot on the road. Then when the Lisbon-Lyon route came up we saw even less of each other. I met a Ukrainian woman refugee in Braga where I made regular stops and one thing led to another. She relies on me for financial support. When I heard about Maria being dead, I knew she would never never hang herself. She was afraid of heights. In fact she was afraid of life...."

He began to sob, a little boy in a big man's body. Janvier and I remained silent in sympathy. The man was either a brilliant actor or he was genuine. Eventually I broke the silence by saying gently, "You said it was your idea to go into police custody."

Janvier cut in before he could answer. "Actually it was my chief's idea. He now agrees with me the murder must be the work of the Albanians. He thought that if the Albanians thought they were safe they would relax, give themselves away. It would also give us more time to get the evidence against them and recover the Shroud. Monsieur O'Mara is – in the time honoured phrase - helping us with enquiries." He said this in such a way that made me think he was not entirely in agreement with the idea. His boss still seemed to want a quick solution as he had when he had been willing to accept Maria's death was suicide.

"I admit that we need more time," Janvier continued, as if he had read my thoughts. "If we are to make the link with the Shroud and find out what they did with it, we need them to make a move. When we explained the plan to Monsieur Mara, he agreed to be in protective custody."

"Does that mean he is not under arrest?" I asked.

"No, he is not. We will put out a statement that the focus of further investigations has moved to Portugal. We will not name the person helping us, in other words the suspect, and hope the media don't dig too deeply. Fortunately our yellow press are more constrained than your British ones. Meantime as Maria's next of kin, Finbar will stay in the flat with Inspector Marty in the second bedroom and clear out his wife's things from the concierge flat. What is not his, will go to her parents. It is extremely unlikely that the Shroud or the Albanians will be showing up here, so you will both be safe. I need not stress that you have learned all this in the strictest confidence. If you break that, you will find yourself in real trouble. Protective custody works two ways. We protect you from the bad guys and we protect you from yourselves". He looked at me. "So carry on as if you know nothing. OK?"

"There is something I have to tell you, Commissaire. I hope you will not be angry. Have you considered that the lorry the Albanians use may have a hidden compartment in which they could have brought the Shroud chest through customs?"

He stared at me but the annoyance I expected did not come. "Go on."

I told him about the voices I heard on the Tuesday night when the lorry was being loaded and that they could have been an instruction to open or use a secret compartment. I said that I had asked one of my students to take a look at the Brocando premises and see if he could spot the lorry. I told him Guiliano reckoned there was a wall a metre short of the back of the cab. I massaged the story to omit that I had been there too.

"Thank you. We suspected there was something like that. It will help when we need a search warrant but we're not there yet. They are not keeping the Shroud there. The cameras I have in and around Brocando will probably have picked up your lad, so I'll take a look."

Oh dear, they will have caught me on camera too. Well, it was too late now. I would wait for my scolding but as I had given him a piece of good information I doubted he could be too displeased. The two men had finished their wine, but declined another glass and left. I re-heated my meal.

What a bizarre situation. Whether Janvier liked it or not I was determined to stay involved. On one level I felt sympathy for him. His boss seemed to be interfering in unhelpful ways, or was the boss he spoke about perhaps not a senior policeman but a *juge d'instruction*, the investigating magistrate in the French system? One of them called Comeliau had given Maigret huge grief in the Simenon stories. I could just imagine the prissy Comeliau behaving in this way. I suppose O'Mara was lucky he had not ordered the Irishman to be really put behind bars. Janvier was apparently also under constraint from the Narcotic squad or Interpol to keep watching the Albanians and not bring them in for questioning. Maybe I should have been more grateful that I was being protected and that he had shared with me as much as he did. Especially as I had ignored his instruction to desist from poking my nose into the case. Frankly, I had become energised and obsessed with it.

Chapter 13

It was my second weekend in Paris and I needed to make another trip to Auchan to re-stock my larder. With Brocando locked and deserted, it was considered safe by our protectors for me to take the metro out to La Defense as the gang were unlikely to return to the crime scene. I called on Finbar and Inspector Marty on my return to invite them to share a meal with me *chez moi* later that evening, but Marty had gone, to be replaced by another of the PJ team. The new policeman declined the invitation in favour of a football game that was shown on television. Finbar accepted readily as he had already finished his task of clearing out Maria's belongings. Sadly, she had a meagre wardrobe and little jewellery.

I made a bolognaise sauce and a white sauce; layering them into a baking tin with a packet of pasta sheets, and popped my lasagne in the oven while I chopped up the ingredients of a green salad. The selection of cheeses (on which I had spent a fortune) served as a second course accompanied by a bunch of grapes. It wasn't Masterchef stuff but I enjoy cooking and Finbar was most appreciative.

"Most lorry drivers are too fat from sitting on their arses and eating junk food or sitting in fast food joints on the road, but I'm well trained. Maria, God rest her soul, and Olga my Ukrainian lady both were strict with my eating. They taught me to stay out of the junk food stuff. Maria was big on fish, being Portuguese. Olga is a veggie but when I want a steak I can get one on the road."

I asked him to tell me a bit more about himself and I reciprocated. He relaxed (perhaps too much) as the bottle of Fitou was depleted.

"You know, it's funny sitting here with an English fella. My father was in the Provos and when I was a bit of a rebel in my teens I did a wee bit meeself. All in the past now and I'm glad about that." He laughed. "All in the past now. Good Friday agreement and all that. And the statute of limitations. Even those buggers who did Bloody Sunday are pardoned. It's like the bloody priest giving you absolution and then putting his hand down your shorts."

I wondered if this obvious distaste for priests and the Catholic Church was a factor in his estrangement from Maria. Ireland had seen a huge decline in support for the Church after the pedophile scandals. However, the last thing I wanted was to get in a discussion on religion or his marriage. Or worst of all, the Anglo-Irish dance of death through the past century, so I diverted him by asking if he found anything in Maria's apartment that might help the police.

"Not much. I found her mobile phone down the back of an armchair. I am surprised the police didn't take it. Probably they couldn't find it. Battery was flat but I recharged it. Do you think I should hand it over?"

I said that he probably should but it gave me another idea. "Can I see it, please?" He handed it over and went to the toilet. There was no passcode. Another instance of Maria's naivety. I quickly opened the Contacts app and looked down the list. Several numbers beginning +351 were obviously family or friends in Portugal. The occupants of the apartment block were listed by name and flat number. I saw that the former tenants of my flat, the McKinleys had both a landline and a French mobile. There were a few Paris numbers like doctor, hairdresser and a couple of female names. It was heart-breaking to see how few contacts she had in her phone, She must have been very lonely after Finbar had left. I felt myself on the brink of tears. Then I found it. It was under 'Brocando' and listed the two premises and a mobile for 'Graziano'. I took down the number and handed the phone back to Finbar. A cunning plan, or was it crazy idea had come into my mind but it would require the help of the Irishman. He looked at me, his eyes full of tears.

"Was it there in the WC, from that wee window that you saw the rope?"

I nodded. "How much do you want to nail this Albanian guy, Finbar?"

"More than you can think. I told you I felt feckin' guilty and I feckin' do. I should have helped her to get out of this shitty place. If I meet this guy before the police get him, he's a dead man. I have a souvenir of my Provo days that will settle the score."

I suspected his souvenir was a firearm but did not want to pursue the matter. We had reached a point where I knew it was time to terminate the discussion until I could properly think through my plan of action which would require his help and perhaps even his firearm. I showed Finbar out and asked him to come tomorrow morning at eleven when I would let him know what I had in mind.

"Use the wooden stair at the back and knock on my kitchen door. OK?" As he went upstairs I could hear the football still blaring from the telly in the flat above.

Chapter 14

I got up early and slipped out of the flat. Brocando had put a notice on the door advising any potential customers that from now on, the business had been transferred to the shop near the Sorbonne and a different landline was listed from the one in Maria's phone. I could see through the shop window that already most of the furniture had been moved out. It crossed my mind that they might have twigged the police surveillance and were preparing to flee before the police closed in. I hoped that my plan of action would be in time and that Graziano and the Shroud were still in Paris. After a café and croissants in the Gare du Nord, I called Nick the train steward.

"Are you working today?"

"No. I'm off but I go to church on Sundays. Want to come?"

"No thanks but I have some lasagne left from last night and I thought you might like it. Can I leave it in your room?"

"Be my guest. I leave it open anyway. Nothing worth stealing except the gold bars under the bed."

"Thanks. I'll put it in your fridge."

I got what I wanted at a small shop run by Magreban immigrants near the Gare du Nord and returned to the apartments in Rue Marronnier. The crime scene tape had been removed from the top of the cellar stairs but our guardian was still in the Adam flat and the surveillance system was still operating inside my flat. Just after eleven I heard two taps on my kitchen door. I opened it and stepped outside, squeezing past Finbar on the narrow stair and locking the door behind me. I was carrying the lasagne in a plastic box.

"Oh," he said. "Are we off somewhere?"

I pointed up the stair. "Is your police guard still in the flat?"

"Yup. His team lost so he's having a long lie."

He was probably not watching my flat but it was better to be on the safe side.

I beckoned Finbar to follow and we climbed to the attic floor. The nurse was on duty and the Romanian student still away. I pushed open the door of Nick's little room and we squeezed in. I put the plastic box in his tiny fridge which had very little else in it. The Irishman stood looking at me as if I had gone crazy. I motioned him to sit down on the bed and shut the door.

"Sorry about this but my flat is bugged. For my own protection of course." I smiled. "Here we can talk without being overheard. You said you would do anything to get the guy who killed Maria?" He nodded. "We both know it was the Albanian and I know that Janvier thinks that too. Do you agree?" Another nod. "OK. There's no way that the police will let us in on what's happening. They're waiting for him to make a move with the Shroud and catch him with it. So we have to find him ourselves."

"And how are WE going to do that? Wave a magic wand?"

"I am going to contact him on his mobile number which I got from Maria's contacts."

"And say to him 'I know you did the murders. Why don't you come and murder me too?' Max, you're off yer feckin' head. He'll either come and knock ye off, or you'll spook him and Janvier will go bananas and this time we both will be really in the pokey."

"I intend to do something that the police can't do officially. I am going to pose as a billionaire who wants to buy the Shroud from him. Has he ever met you? Does he know what you look like?"

"No."

"No pictures in Maria's flat, like a wedding picture?"

"Only the Virgin Mary and I don't think I look like her." He was beginning to be less hostile. "You want me to pose as John Magnier?" He pronounced it 'Magneer'.

"Who's he?"

"He's a billionaire who's bought up most of the land for sale in Ireland. You're not a turf man or you'd know his name. He's better known than the Arabs in the stud business. Got a huge stud farm in Coolmore near to my calf country. The newspapers call him the bloodstock tycoon."

"Well, he sounds ideal if you are playing the part, but I

had you in mind more as my bodyguard."

"I can do that alright with my wee Provo pistol. But what if he recognises you as the Englishman who lives in Maria's flats? Or the guy that spotted him in Turin?"

"Well, I'm pretty sure he didn't see me in Turin but he did see me in the cellars. So I have to get myself a disguise. And an accent. I actually have someone in mind to model myself on. I found him on the internet after you left last night. I'll tell you who he is in a minute. But this is not going to be easy. There are three of them in the gang. Maybe we just find out where he is holding the Shroud, tell the police and duck out."

"I've got good news on that score, Max. Two of the Albanians have gone off to Italy with their lorry, packed with furniture. I heard the police guy I'm sharing with, being told that last night on the phone. He was annoyed about being interrupted in his football game and he wasn't being too careful about me overhearing the call. Apparently they crossed at Modane and there were definitely only two of them. Janvier had them search the van and I think they even opened the secret compartment and found it empty."

"Hopefully it means the Shroud is still in Paris with the boss man. It would be really smart to double back and take it into Italy but something tells me that's not what's happening. More likely they are divesting themselves of the furniture, selling the Shroud and escaping. They know there's a murder hunt and the longer they stay here the more chance the police will get evidence to charge them."

"Selling that Shroud thing is not going to be easy, Max."

"Unless there already is a buyer and the Shroud was stolen to order. A lot of the luxury cars that are stolen in London are stolen to order and shipped off to Eastern Europe. Why not the Shroud?"

"Yes, but who's gonna buy it? The Vatican to get it back? It's not as if someone is gonna to be nutty enough to buy it to hang it on their wall."

"If it were the Vatican there would have been a ransom demand before now. Your idea about the nutter is wrong though. There are nutters rich enough and daft enough to buy famous art and hang it on their wall. The man I have in mind is a religious nutter who has already paid millions for religious relics. He has billions to do it and lucky for me he is a recluse. No one has seen him in public for years and if the Albanian checks up on him, this man's mansion won't take his call. He has a private jet so he could easily have come to France to collect the Shroud. He would not be intending to put it on display. Instead he would hang it at his home and use it for some kind of personal devotion."

"Who is this guy?"

"He's a Croatian-American called Milo Havranic. Made his fortune in the Silicon Valley dot.com boom then switched to mining precious metals before the boom in electric cars saw the prices take off. He's autistic and deeply Catholic."

"What's the difference?" Finbar jibed.

Now was not the time to get into his agenda with the Irish Catholic church so I pursued to outline my plan.

"Bizarrely he was also a friend of Mother Theresa and

supported her cause for canonisation. The last time he was seen in public was in St Peter's Rome when she was made a saint. Since then he has become a recluse. It's said he prays through Mother Theresa and lives like a monk."

"Funny sort of monk who's a billionaire."

"Indeed. He was asked if he supported charity and he quoted a verse from the Bible about doing good in ways that nobody sees. So nobody knows. His staff all have to sign strict confidentiality agreements. The last (and only) one who broke this and gave an interview to a newspaper was slapped with a super injunction. She was a housekeeper at his estate and he sued her. The poor woman was bankrupted and committed suicide. That didn't exactly *encourager les autres.*"

"Doesn't sound like a guy the Albanian could do business with."

"Funny you should say that. You know what nationality Mother Theresa was?"

"You're gonna tell me."

"Albanian."

"How did ya get all dis stuff?"

"Wikipedia. It had a few pictures of him before he became a recluse. He's my height and he had a wispy little beard and wore tinted glasses. I reckon I could get fitted with a fake beard, tinted glasses and look the part."

"Ah, but can you sound the part?"

"You have a point. There are two interviews with him on YouTube from ten years ago. Thankfully he sounds

American not Croatian. His parents went to the USA after the second World War and he was born there. In Alabama. He went to Caltec for university and never went back. You can still hear traces of the Deep South but I'll have to practise. Are you on board?"

"Sure, but where are we headed?"

"I will call him and say that I know he has the Shroud. I'll say I hired a detective agency and spoke to some Albanians (whom I will refuse to name). I will make him an offer bigger than what he was paid to take it. I'm assuming that he either has a buyer in mind or was commissioned. But first I need to see the Shroud and assure myself that he has it. That's the bait and if we can get him to meet us we'll tip off the police."

"Seems good to me. What if he traces your call?"

"I bought a burner phone this morning near the station. I will use it to call him and if we get a meet, I'll use it to let Janvier know, anonymously of course. Let's go. The guy who stays in this room will be back soon. I have to go and practise my American accent."

Finbar stopped in the narrow corridor outside Nick's room and turned. "Oh by the way, the police fella says I can go back to Lyon and pick up my lorry tomorrow or the day after. They think we're no longer needing protection and I'm no longer under arrest unofficially or not. So presumably you are going to do this soon. Like tomorrow?"

I wondered if Janvier and the other police involved had decided to move in on the Albanians. But even if they did there was no harm in putting my plan into action today. It would have been nice if they had let me know my own 'witness protection' time was up. Or maybe it wasn't. Janvier had been clear they would need me in any trial. I was more concerned with where I could get a false beard.

First things first. The phone call. I went into the flat, wrote down some phrases, tried them out on my own phone and listened back. I was going to talk in English to someone who was Albanian and operated between Italy and France. He would not be suspicious if my American accent was not perfect. If I had to switch to French I would overlay it with American pronunciation to disguise my own.

I walked round to Rue Rochechouart and up it until I came on a little park with a children's playground that was far enough away from traffic noise of Boulevard Rochechouard up ahead. On an unoccupied bench I sat down and took out my burner phone and my notes. He answered after two rings and before I could speak he said in French, "Who is this? Who gave you this number?"

I was sure it was him so I launched into my story. "I know you have the Shroud. My name is Milo Havranic, an American citizen. You can look me up on Wikipedia. I am in Paris. Do you speak English?"

There was a long pause until he said cautiously, "Yes, I speak English. What do you want?"

"I want to buy it. I'll give you more than the people who asked you to steal it if you haven't handed it over already. I take it that it's still for sale."

Another long pause. "Who did you say you are?"

"I am Milo Havranic. I am American and I want to buy the Shroud. Look me up. You will see I have money. I need you to name a price but first I want to be sure you still have it. I want to see it. I want to meet and I haven't much time. My private jet is at Le Bourget and I need to fly to London on Tuesday. When can we meet? And where?"

My tactic was based on the fact that big money people usually want what they want quickly and in general ask more questions than they volunteer answers. Another pause.

"If you are who you say you are, I will need to check. I will phone you back in an hour. But first you must answer me a question. How did you get this number? Who told you about me?"

I had prepared for this.

"When I read the Shroud was missing I hired a detective agency in Milan. They have contacts in Interpol who told me the police think the Shroud is in Paris, hidden somewhere. My agency made enquiries about you and your business. We know you are linked to Albania. So am I because I had a very good friend from Albania. I think you may know her as Teresa Bojaxhiu."(I pronounced it [bɔjaˈdʒiu]). "I know her as Mother Theresa".

I was certain he would know exactly who she was even if the guy was probably an atheist. I concluded that not only because he was a criminal but because until recently Albania was the only officially atheist country in Europe. It was his greed not his beliefs I was appealing to.

"Go on," he said quietly.

I was thrilled he had not hung up on me so far. Naturally he had not admitted he had the Shroud. He was not daft. He was not going to open up on a cold call from someone he did not know. I was sure also that he would suspect the police were watching Brocando and him, whether or not he had believed the announcement that Maria's husband was in custody. I had to allow him to dictate where and when we would meet, if anything to make him feel secure.

"You tell me when and where I can meet you. Meanwhile. Check me out."

I hung up. The sting had begun. All the stuff about Havranic's obsession with religious relics and Mother T were on Wikipedia. I hoped he would take it at face value and not dig too deeply.

A frustrating hour passed until the burner phone rang.

"Where are you staying?" he asked. Oh dear, I had not thought of that. I had to think fast and I did not know many good hotels in Paris other than the famous ones. "George Cinq" I said without hesitating, knowing that this could possibly cost me an arm and a leg if I had to book into this luxury hotel. The fees for my summer courses gone in a night. Maybe if we got the Shroud back there would be a reward. "I check out tomorrow at noon. I need to be in London by six," I added, knowing I could not afford a few days in the George Cinq waiting for a phone call that might not come. "For security I never book in my own name. It will be under Kaplan."

"Wait there this afternoon. You will get a message. I will

call you again on this number to confirm the arrangements"
He disconnected.

I now had an expensive dilemna. A quick internet search showed that rooms at the George V which is between the Champs Elysees and the Madeleine started at 2500 euros per night. I called them.

"Hotel George Cinq. Bonjour."

"I'm calling on behalf of Mr George Kaplan. I'm his agent in Paris. Do you have a room for tonight? I don't need a suite. It's an emergency as his private jet is landing at Le Bourget soon and he needs to know where he is staying."

"I think we can accommodate him, sir. A superior room at two and half thousand euros per night. Will that be satisfactory? Has he stayed here previously? Then we need Payment by credit card in advance." I swallowed hard.

"That's fine. He will be in about an hour to check in. I don't have his card just at hand. Can you wait an hour?" I boldly lied.

I quickly phoned upstairs to Finbar and told him to get himself to a room where we couldn't be overheard.

"Listen. It's going better than I thought. But I need you to run round in the best clothes you have with you to the Hotel George Cinq. Go to the check in desk and tell them that you are waiting for Mr George Kaplan. He'll be there soon. Buy yourself a coffee on me. Where are you now?"

"Sitting on the lavvy. You said to go to one of the blind spots."

"OK, see you there in an hour. Remember I'm going to be

called George Kaplan. Oh, and bring your Provo friend with you."

"Roger Casement as we say in Ireland."

I was now in a lather, more about being escorted out of the George Cinq for failing to provide my credit card than I was about my non-existent beard. Or tinted glasses. The latter I could pick up at any tourist kiosk in the Champs Elysées area. But the beard? I ran up the stairs and knocked at Myriam Boudienne's door. She opened up and looked surprised.

"Hello. I'm Max Quillan. I took the McKinley's flat on the second floor. I am having a little cocktail party end of this week for those who stay in this apartment. I thought it might cheer everyone up after the terrible murders. I thought I'd start with you as you work usually through *l'heure de l'aperitif* and ask which night would suit you. That's if you want to come?"

"What a great idea," she smiled, a wide smile that showed a set of perfect white teeth. "I won't be working this Friday and I'd love to come." Provided Nick was not riding the rails on Friday I was sure he would be over the moon. There was no question of him not wanting to come.

"I wonder if I might ask your advice on something else," I continued. "I am going to a strange social event this evening organised by friends of mine. We all have to wear a false beard or grow one, but it's too late for that, and the ladies who are coming get to vote on the winner. I thought of going with a little goatee beard."

She tossed back her long black hair and roared with

laughter. "Don't tell me, you want to borrow some clippings of my hair! I'm always getting letters about it. Some of them are bit fetishist!" Another roar of laughter.

"Well no, but I wondered if you knew of somewhere that might be open this afternoon where they could sell me a false beard or make me up to look as if I had one?"

"Alas no. All the hairdressers and theatrical shops will be closed. But I'll do it for you. I am not really a *Metéo* expert at all. I'm an actress and I just read on the television what they write for me. I'm just a pretty face as you English say. I have a full make-up set in my bathroom and I'll give you a little goatee with some spirit gum. But I have to go our in an hour so it will have to be now."

"More than perfect," I replied.

She took me through to her bathroom which was an Aladdin's cave of potions and creams, sat me down at the wash hand basin and opened a cupboard. "Do you want a wispy moustache to go with it?"

"Yes please."

She got to work by cutting some of my hair at the back of head which was the same salt and pepper grey as the pictures of Milo Havranic on the internet, and sticking these to my face with spirit gum. I hurried back to my flat, grabbed a white panama hat and went to look for a taxi. I was lucky and was soon on my way when the burner phone rang.

"Are you there?"

"My messenger said you had not yet checked in. If you are who you say you are, pick up the message at the desk. If not fuck off. I have a buyer and I don't need this hassle."

"I'm sorry. I had to go into the centre. I will be there in ten minutes."

"Ten minutes, that's all. The rendezvous is at six this evening or not at all." He cut the call.

Chapter 15

Luck was running with me. Not just with the beard but the fact he was in a hurry to close a deal. Perhaps he was going to play me off against the mystery buyer. But it was all happening too quickly. The taxi waited while I bought some blue tinted glasses at a kiosk and dropped me at the hotel.

I could see Finbar lolling in a chair in the lobby but I went straight to the reception, almost forgetting to speak like an American.

"I'm very sorry. My name is George Kaplan. I made a reservation by phone and my agent over there. The man in the yellow jacket. He came to say I would be delayed. I'm very sorry for your trouble but I find I have to return to Le Bourget immediately and cancel my room." I slid a fifty euro note across the counter."That's for your trouble. By chance, are there any messages for me? I am expecting one."

The clerk raised an eyebrow. I wasn't sure if that meant he was thinking that I was an imposter, which of course I was. Or it was a way of acknowledging I had tipped for services which had not been rendered.

"There is a message, sir. We kept it until your arrival." He handed me a small cheap brown envelope. Inside was a small scrap of paper.

"Thank you."

I turned and read the note as I walked towards O'Mara. It said in capitals: 'RUSSIAN ORTHODOX CATHEDRAL OF HOLY TRINITY QUAI BRANLY. WAIT INSIDE FOR THE WOMAN IN RED DRESS. IF NOT THERE BY SIX, FO'

I motioned to O'Mara that we were leaving. I made for the concierge desk and asked for a taxi in my best American accent. We got one waiting outside the hotel and I gave the address on the note. It wasn't far. Just over Pont d'Alma on the Left Bank, and visible by the silver onion domes as we crossed the bridge.

"What's the story?" Finbar wanted to know. "Is he going to meet us?"

"I don't know. We have to look for a woman in a red dress. Obviously he's being careful to see if we have the police with us."

"Why do I think that George Kaplan is familiar?" Finbar asked.

"Ever seen Hitchcock's film 'North by North West'?" It took a moment before his face lit up.

"You cheeky bugger! He's the man who booked the hotel rooms in that name. The bad guys thought Cary Grant was him, but he didn't exist!"

"Exactly. We got away with it and it only cost me fifty

euros as a tip to get the message. If I'd had to check in there they would have squeezed my credit card for two and half thousand and it would have bounced. We would have been out on the pavement with no message."

The building to which we were headed was new to me. When I had last been in Paris the main Russian Orthodox church was the Cathedral of St Alexander Nevsky beside Parc Monceau, consecrated in 1861. In 1922 it became a Cathedral church frequented by those who wanted nothing to do with Soviet Russia. In the long and fissiparous history of Orthodoxy it was hard to keep up with all the splits.

Holy Trinity Cathedral where we were headed on the other side of the Seine, represented an attempt by the Russian Orthodox to woo Paris anew in the years of Putin power when the Church was back in favour in Russia. It heartily supported all of Putin's policies (including the war on Ukraine).

The new Cathedral is an eye-catching blend of traditional onion domes and modern styles and adjoins a Spiritual and Cultural Centre. In addition, separate buildings in a nearby part of Paris house an educational complex and an administrative building. Paris has never shrunk from embracing bold new architecture. The investment has paid off for both sides. Despite their links to Putin the Moscow Patriachate was welcomed by the Mayor of Paris at the opening in March 2016. As a public relations exercise the investment proved to be a winner. The Cathedral was one of the most visited places during the Days of the French

National Heritage festival held in 2017 when more than 12,000 people went through its doors.

There were a lot less today inside the Cathedral. It would not have been hard to spot a lady in a red dress but no such person was in sight. I had still not phoned Janvier as I had no idea what I could tell him. 'Come to the Orthodox cathedral, we think the Shroud is here!' It was not yet credible and we would just have to wait until we had a lead. We stood looking around when a tall, bearded man in black military fatigues came up behind us and asked fiercely "Are you Havranic?" I nodded.

"Follow me," he grunted. He led us out of the main church down a passage and through a door. I saw that he had badges on his upper arms. One was a circle with a skull inside, the insignia on the other arm was a gold star with cyrillic script which I could not make out.

I guessed we were now in the Cultural Centre adjoining the cathedral. We walked down a corridor suffused with the smell of new paint. Art work hung in gallery-style rooms on either side of the corridor. We went through two more doors until we came to one marked 'private'. Another security guard stood inside with the same insignia on his black uniform. Then I remembered what it signified. They were from the infamous Wagner group of mercenaries, the shock troops which had played such a significant part in Ukraine and were also guns for hire in African countries where the Kremlin had ambitions. The tough guy inside the door fleeced us for weapons while the one who had brought us from the church looked on, his automatic weapon held in both hands. When his colleague found Finbar's Provo pistol, he cocked his weapon to keep us covered. My cunning plan had turned out rather differently from what I had envisaged. To put it bluntly I was shit scared. I could do nothing about it now and would have to carry on with my scheme or own up and end up in the Seine.

Finbar's gun unsurprisingly was confiscated and we were led into a large room. The Wagner men stood on either side of the door behind us. In the centre stood the silver and wood chest containing the Turin Shroud. Behind it was a tall rotund figure in a black cassock with a pudgy pink face. He had gimlet eyes and a wispy little beard that looked as genuine as mine. To the side stood 'Graziano' the Albanian. The tall priest turned to him and asked,"Is this Mister Havranic?" I thought I heard the whisper of a stammer. There was something familiar about this man.

The Albanian said he had never met Havranic but I looked like the internet picture and when he saw me on CCTV come into the cathedral he was sure it was the right man. I could tell he was nervous. The arrogant leer was gone and he looked pale. He was not in control of this meeting. The priest was. It suddenly became clear to me that the Orthodox people were the intended buyers of the Shroud, and perhaps even had commissioned the theft. The Albanian's greed had led him to think he could screw more money by making this into an auction. In falling for my ploy, it now looked as if he found himself on the wrong side of the Orthodox people who did not look pleased. The priest turned to me.

"Perhaps you would be so good as to confirm that you are the one who phoned this man..and you told him you knew he had the Shroud...and offered him more than we were paying him. How...did you know...that we were paying him?" The stammer was now more evident. I remembered then who he was and where I had seen him before.

"I did not know of your involvement, I swear to you," I replied, continuing in my American accent, praying that he would not remember that we had met previously at a conference in Moscow. "I hired private detectives and they had inside track to Interpol. They had identified this man. My people found him in Paris and reckoned he was about to sell the Shroud. So I came over on my plane and made him an offer. He told me to come here. See, that's my invitation." I thrust out the little piece of paper the *George Cinq* had given me. I could feel the changes in my nervous system that people under interrogation exhibit. What was going to happen if they found out I was a fake?

"You said you made an offer. What offer?"

"Well nothing yet. Until I know what you are offering I'm not buying. But I am interested in doing a deal."

"You are in no position to do any deal. You have no business here. Who is this man?" he looked at Finbar.

"He is working for me. Security. That's why he had a gun." I jumped in with the answer before Finbar could put his foot in his big Irish mouth. To my relief, it seemed they were not interested in him after that.

"Very well. I suppose I should introduce myself. I am Archpriest Vsevolod Chaplin of the Moscow Patriarchate. We commissioned this Albanian to acquire the Shroud for us. Why did you want it? What were you going to do with it?" I noted the past tense. He held the winning cards.

I gave him the line of being a rich man but explained that I was also a devout Christian. Jesus had told us that it was difficult for a rich man to reach heaven and so I wanted to have the Shroud close to me to inspire me. It was something I would keep privately in my own home."

He actually laughed. "You Americans think that you own the world. Or you can buy it. Far from being Christian you are destroying it with homosexuality and pedophilia. The Roman Catholic church is full of it. As for L..G..B..T..Q," he stammered the letters as if he were spitting them. "You no longer are a 'Nation under God' as you are fond of saying. It is left to us in Russia to keep the flame of true Christianity alive in the Orthodox religion."

Now I know that the real Milo Havranic would probably have taken issue with this, as a born-again Christian and an American patriot, even if he was now a recluse. But I was not going to get into an argument with Chaplin. You see I knew the man and I had better explain how.

In 2014 I had attended a historical conference in Moscow at which Chaplin was prominent as a host. He then headed up the Church and Society department of the Moscow Patriarchate of the Orthodox Church and was well-known as the right hand man of the Patriarch Kirill. When Kirill became Patriarch in 2009 with Putin's blessing, it was natural that his protége's career would prosper. The two of them went back at least twenty years and often Chaplin would be the mouthpiece for hardline conservative statements on moral and social issues, including his support for Russian intervention in Syria and Ukraine.

He had once said that "traitors" deserved to die. I'm not sure if he meant heretics who deserted the Orthodox faith or unpatriotic Russians. His email address was 'vodkafans2000' and he enjoyed winding up western church figures.

My own meeting with him was at a reception at the historical conference when he told an audience that in the Orthodox tradition if a church went on fire and if there was a choice between saving the icons or the people inside, "We always save the icons!"

I remember thinking at the time this had more than a ring of truth, when applied to incidents like the Kursk sinking and the Nord-Ost theatre seige. I had been a keynote speaker at the conference because there was a lot of similarity to what happened in Russia in the thirteenth century and the crusade against the Cathars in the same period. In the 13th century Kievan Rus (the cradle of Russian Christianity) was overwhelmed by the Mongolian invasion. The Tatar Yoke fell over the land when Khan Batu, a grandson of the Mongolian conqueror Ghengis Khan, led the four hundred thousand horsemen of the Golden Horde into the Russian lands in 1237. The Kievan state collapsed in 1240. Alexander Nevsky the warrior saint knew that he couldn't beat the

Tatars so he did a deal in paying them tribute. The Orthodox believers survived and eventually bounced back. The opposite fate befell the Cathars in France who were all wiped out.

But that's enough history. Rather than argue with Chaplin, I asked what he had in mind for the Shroud.

"To put it on public display, of course. The moral decline of the West has given us an opportunity to act as a beacon for true devotion. We will put it in the Cathedral of Christ the Saviour in Moscow and allow people to see it. It is one of the most important icons in the world. It does not belong in the hands of Western Churches or a decayed civilisation."

The church site in Moscow he had in mind had been blown up by Stalin, turned into an open-air swimming pool by Krushchev, then rebuilt with no expense spared as a church by Yeltsin who had extorted the money from oligarchs to build it.

I was not going to ask Chaplin whether he accepted that the Shroud was genuine. Or if he was uneasy about the fact it had been stolen. The fact that it was stolen property was not going to put off Putin, Kirill or anyone else in the Kremlin. They seemed to relish playing the bad guys on the world stage and the sanctions of the West only made them more popular in their own country. All I wanted was to get out of there as soon as possible.

"OK so it's not for sale. I accept I made a mistake. I'm sorry. We will leave you."

All this time I had been looking at Chaplin and not the

Albanian. I now saw that Graziano was clearly ill at ease. He had completely lost control of the situation and worse was about to come.

Chaplin ignored my intention to leave and turned to address 'Graziano'.

The stammer had disappeared. "Your greed in bringing in the American is bad enough. But to have betrayed us who trusted you is worse. Your woman in the red dress who came to the cathedral has been sent away. In Albania I know that people who betray their family know what to expect. In Russia we also know what to do with traitors." He nodded at one of the Wagner men who was wearing black gloves. He took out the gun he had confiscated from Finbar and shot the Albanian twice in the chest.

Graziano slumped to his knees, head bowed, and the militiaman stepped forward and shot him again through the back of his head so that the blood spattered on the floor tiles. I opened my mouth to protest but could not speak. Were Finbar and I to be next?

The Wagner men approached Finbar. One pointed a gun at his back. The other grabbed his hand and wrapped Finbar's fingers around the stock of the 'Provo' gun. He was wearing gloves and when he reclaimed the gun I began to understand what was being planned. They were about to set us up as the killers. They pushed Finbar towards where I was standing and nodded to Chaplin.

"I'm sorry you had to witness that. But that gun is our insurance policy. If either of you speak of what you have seen here today I have two witnesses who will say that you shot this man when you found he would not sell you the Shroud. The gun will be put in a plastic bag and kept here. If you tell anyone, it will find its way to the French police. They will already have found his body where we will leave it and if you say anything about what happened here today we will tell them where to find you. You will be welcome to come and see the Shroud in Moscow. *Poka*!"

With that he turned and went out a door behind him. The Wagner militiamen escorted us back through the corridors to a side door which they unlocked and pushed us out. Finbar was grinning. A silly grin, that probably owed more to relief than happiness.

"BeeJesus! That priest was some fella. At least he doesn't like paedophiles, even he is a killer. Can't say I feel exactly sorry for that Albanian bastard. I'd have shot him myself if I had the chance."

I gulped the fresh air. "Let's get out of here. I need a drink."

We walked across the Pont d'Alma and found a bar. I ordered a large vodka and spilled some on my palm with which to clean off the spirit gum holding my beard in place. Should I phone Janvier? Perhaps I should simply say nothing and be glad to have survived. Janvier would know soon enough that 'Graziano' was dead and when the Russians unveiled the Shroud in Moscow he would know who took it.

Epilogue

In the event it was Janvier who phoned me on Monday evening to arrange a meeting. When I got there he looked relaxed.

"I thought I should update you that we found 'Graziano's' body in the Bois de Boulogne early this morning. He had been shot three times by the same gun. Fortunately the bullets were in the body so if we find the weapon we may get the killer but usually after professional kills like this the gunman dumps the weapon in the Seine. Our Italian colleagues have arrested the brother and cousin in Italy and we are currently getting extradition warrants for them in case they try to skip to Albania. The woman who worked at the Brocando shop in Rue Marronnier has agreed to give statements in the case we sent to the magistrate on the furniture and drug smuggling racket. You may have seen her in the shop. Often wears a bright red dress." He looked at me as if he expected me to say something.

"As I think you know Maria's husband went back to Lyon, collected his lorry and is on the road again. We dropped the surveillance of you on Sunday."

"Sunday? Was that after you found the body of the killer?"

"No. We didn't find that until Monday but we were sure you weren't in any more danger Mr Kaplan. Sorry I mean Mr Quillan." Another pause and a meaningful look.

"But we did have your back when you were in the Russian Orthodox Cathedral. Two of our officers followed you and Mr O'Mara into the Cultural Centre and waited until you came out."

"Why did they not intervene?"

"Sometimes justice gets done in strange ways. I don't think anyone will argue Graziano's death will be any great loss. Lots of people will say '*grazie*' for us holding back. As for the box in that room, we didn't have a search warrant. It's probably in Moscow by now anyway. I thought you didn't believe it was the genuine thing anyway, so whoever has it has bought a pig in a poke. If that's not too blasphemous."

"We could have been killed by the Wagner people" I objected petulantly.

He looked at me with a steely expression. "You mean we failed to intervene to stop you doing something we told you not to do, but did by free choice anyway? In any case it wasn't you in that cathedral anyway. It was an American billionaire." He was playing with me and I knew it.

So I forgave him and invited him to my murder mystery cocktail party. He came, as did Myriam, and the Fischers. Madame Lafont declined and naturally I didn't invite Dieudonné in case he came. Duchamps and the couple from Gers were still away. The nurse from Sierra Leone came for a while on her way to a night shift. Nick of course was there and was predictably star-struck by Myriam. It made his summer. I didn't invite any of my students - there was time enough for that.

As for winners and losers: Janvier was able to close his case and shut down the Albanian crime trio. There was tragedy and death for poor Maria and a brutal end to the loveless life of Madam Adam. The Russians got a bargain for the 'priceless' Shroud as they didn't have to pay the thieves. Finbar saw the killer of his wife get his just desserts. Me? I got a story that I couldn't tell without incriminating myself. Until now.

Author's note

All the characters in this story are fictitious. I lived for a while in an apartment block in Paris rather like Rue Marronnier but have changed the name and that of the furniture shop which adjoined it. I did also work in Turin briefly and while living there joined the queue to see the Shroud. The historical stuff about the thirteenth century is factual, as is the information about the Russian Orthodox premises in Paris.

There was a real Archpriest Vsevolod Chaplin who worked as an aide to Metropolitan (later Patriarch) Kirill and was known for his ultra-conservative views. In 2015 after he made outspoken comments about corruption, he was dismissed from his two key posts. He subsequently gave an interview saying that his mentor Kirill would not last long in his job. Chaplin died suddenly in 2020. Coincidence?